It was th

"Thanks for co⋯⋯⋯⋯⋯⋯⋯⋯ said to Natalie a⋯⋯⋯⋯⋯⋯⋯⋯ his new car.

"Are you kidding? I'm having the time of my life." Natalie turned to him and grinned. She *did* look as if she was having fun. Her long dark hair was whipping in the wind, and fresh air had made Natalie's rosy cheeks a shade pinker than usual. "What else do I need besides you, the sun, and a ride in a yellow convertible?"

His thoughts exactly. Dylan stared at his reflection in the mirrored lenses of Natalie's sunglasses. Tell her now, he commanded himself. . . .

This was the moment he had been waiting for. They were alone, Natalie was happy, and he was driving a brand-new (to him, anyway) convertible. What better time to tell Natalie his true feelings for her?

Dylan cleared his throat. "Actually—"

Don't miss any books in this hot new series:

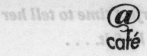

#1 Love Bytes
#2 I'll Have What He's Having
#3 Make Mine to Go
#4 Flavor of the Day

Available from ARCHWAY Paperbacks

@café

I'LL HAVE WHAT HE'S HAVING

by
Elizabeth Craft

AN ARCHWAY PAPERBACK
Published by POCKET BOOKS
New York   London   Toronto   Sydney   Tokyo   Singapore

AN ARCHWAY PAPERBACK *Original*

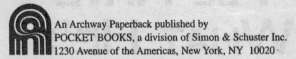

An Archway Paperback published by
POCKET BOOKS, a division of Simon & Schuster Inc.
1230 Avenue of the Americas, New York, NY 10020

Produced by Daniel Weiss Associates, Inc., New York

Copyright © 1997 by Daniel Weiss Associates, Inc., and
Elizabeth Craft
Cover art copyright © 1997 by Daniel Weiss Associates, Inc.

ISBN: 0-671-00446-8

First Archway Paperback printing November 1997

10 9 8 7 6 5 4 3 2

AN ARCHWAY PAPERBACK and colophon are
registered trademarks of Simon & Schuster Inc.

Cover photos taken at DRIP, New York, NY.

Printed in the U.S.A.

IL 7+

In memory of Ellen Craft

Tanya's Star Scape:
Your Astrological Guide

Leo
(July 22–August 22)

I don't know how to break it to all you lions out there, but July just ain't your month. Take heart, though. The stars say the roller coaster better known as your life will improve—eventually. In the meantime here's what you've got to look forward to.

Mood: This month Leos will despair. Every time you think that you've finally made it over that hump we call gloom and doom, you'll find yourself right back in the porcelain throne. But hang in there. By fall you'll have forgotten all those nasty doldrums.

Love: I think the paragraph above says it all. Although many luscious members of the opposite sex think you're the greatest thing since George Clooney or Julianna Margulies on *ER*, the one you love is off watching Ricki Lake when he/she should be pondering how absolutely perfect you are. A word of advice: Be persistent! He/she *will* eventually look under his/her nose and realize (eureka!) that you are *It*.

Friends: On a brighter note, your friends love you. Just like always. Go in for lots of bonding this month. Gossip and general discussions about the Meaning of Life will keep you distracted.

Lucky number: 31

Sara Jane O'Connor (known to everyone under the age of forty as Blue) was suffocating. Well, she wasn't literally suffocating—but the blanket over her head had trapped several million molecules of hot, stuffy air. And now she couldn't breathe. Furthermore, she had no idea what time it was.

Blue didn't immediately throw off her covers. Something—someone— kept her locked in place. She was temporarily paralyzed as the events of the preceding night came rushing back.

She had gone to Matthew Chance's party expecting to meet Shyhunk, the guy Natalie van Lenton and Tanya Childes had set her up with via an Internet personal ad. Natalie and Tanya had insisted that at the mature age of sixteen it was time for Blue to get serious about romance. But Shyhunk hadn't turned out to be a handsome stranger who was going to sweep her off her feet and convince her that romance really *was* a worthy endeavor. Instead Shyhunk turned out to be her very best friend in the whole world, Jason Kirk. After both Jason

ONE

1

and Blue had recovered from the initial shock of realizing that their respective mystery dates were—in fact—each other, they had carried out their evening the way they always did—they had sat in the corner and made fun of everyone else at the party.

The night had flowed by in a pleasant haze of laughter, cruel jokes, and warm diet 7Up. Until later . . .

"Jason?" Blue called out softly. She pushed off the blanket and sat up.

He was gone. The denim beanbag chair in which Jason had fallen asleep the night before was empty. Blue pulled her fingers through her tangled shoulder-length light brown hair. Was it possible that Jason hadn't been there at all? Maybe she had dreamt finding him outside in the middle of the night. . . .

There was no mistaking the sound of someone stumbling around in the back alley behind the pub. Blue had crept downstairs and opened the back door of her family's two-story apartment, expecting to come face-to-face with an ax murderer. Instead she saw Jason's familiar face. In the moonlight his dark blue eyes looked almost black. His shaggy brown hair grazed his collar, highlighting the coral necklace he had worn to the party. Blue gulped as she stared at the tan skin that showed above the neckline of his worn flannel shirt. She was struck by a longing to put her lips gently against that perfect expanse of skin.

"Can I come in?" Jason asked.

Blue nodded. She wasn't sure exactly what she was agreeing to, but she knew the answer was yes. . . .

Blue's heart had pounded as she led Jason up to her room. He had been there a hundred times, but last night his presence had felt different . . . charged. Jason had collapsed onto her beanbag chair, his all-time favorite lounging spot.

"So," Blue said quietly. "What's up?" Her voice was high and breathy. For the first time in her life Blue understood what girls were talking about when in hushed tones they relayed to their friends the moment before The Kiss. In the past her only experience with anything resembling romance had been . . . horrible.

Jason shrugged. "Just your average sleepless night."

Blue nodded. She hadn't been able to sleep, either. Tonight was the first time she had seen Jason as more than a package of arms, legs, and brain. She had seen him as a guy. A guy she might want to kiss. And she had been frightened. And now she was . . . what?

"The party was fun, huh?" Blue asked. The pulse at the base of her neck was fluttering wildly.

He nodded. "I'm glad you were my mystery date," he said.

"I'm glad you were Shyhunk," she responded.

Were her words really as loaded with meaning as they sounded?

Jason settled deeper into the beanbag. His eyes were drooping. "We're a good combo," he said sleepily.

Blue nodded. She was wide awake. In fact, she had never felt more alert in her life. "Yeah," she squeaked.

Jason's eyes were closed now. "Mind if I take a little nap before I go?" he asked.

"No, uh, go ahead." Blue stared at Jason, willing him to say something that would shake her out of this ridiculously romantic frame of mind.

There was nothing between them. She didn't want there to be anything between them. She was just temporarily caught up in the whole teen psycho-romance thing.

But Jason was silent. In fact, he seemed to be sound asleep. "Jason?" Blue called softly. "Jase?"

"Good night, Sara Jane," he murmured. "I love you."

Blue had sat in the dark for hours, stunned by Jason's last three words. She had expected him to wake up and tell her he had been joking. Or something. But he hadn't woken up. And eventually Blue had fallen asleep.

Jason must have finally tiptoed out at the crack of dawn—without a word. Okay. This situation was beyond weird. Blue was in unfamiliar territory. The closest she'd ever been to having a guy sleep in her room was the time in fourth grade when Dan Levy had accidentally sleepwalked in the girls' cabin at Sherwood Forest Camp. Then again, Jason wasn't like a *guy* guy. He was just Jason. *So why was she so freaked?*

Blue glanced at the travel alarm clock that sat on the floor next to her futon mattress. 8:32 A.M. Her parents were probably already at the liquor distributors'. They went there to haggle with Mr. McClarney almost every Saturday morning.

Mr. and Mrs. O'Connor owned The Blarney Stone, an authentic Irish pub that had been Blue's second home for as long as she could remember. Well, technically it was more of a first home since the O'Connors had lived in a two-story apartment over the bar since Blue was born. Both her mom and dad worked seven days a week—they always said there would be plenty of time for rest and relaxation after they were dead.

Thank goodness they weren't home. She felt like being alone. And Jason must have managed to sneak out without parental detection. Otherwise Mrs. O'Connor would have yanked Blue out of deep slumber and given her a lecture about the evils of premarital sex. She never would have believed that a guy could spend the night without anything (anything including kissing, touching, and general groping) happening.

Blue reached over to the pile of dirty

5

clothes next to her mattress and pulled on a faded The Irish Do It Better sweatshirt over the black baby tee that she had worn to bed. She heaved herself into a standing position and walked to her bedroom window. Outside, the day was bright.

She was already starting to feel more like the Blue she had lived with for the last sixteen years. True, she didn't know why Jason had appeared in the middle of the night, but there had to be a reasonable explanation. There had to be. Because she couldn't handle the idea of herself and Jason as a couple.

Blue couldn't let herself forget the last time she had attempted to enter the realm of Eros. Craig Sealy had seemed like a cool guy. He was into poetry, track, and listening to Grateful Dead bootleg tapes. But Craig had turned out to be evil. Way evil. Don't think about it, Blue ordered herself. Don't think about that night. It was too late. The pictures were there, as if Blue had just retrieved them from the One-Hour Photo only blocks from her house.

It had been fall. The air was crisp and textured with the delicious smell of leaves, cut grass, and hot dogs from the concession stand at Alta Vista's first home football game. Of course, that night occurred back when Blue would even *consider* going to a football game. Since then she had sworn off all activities that were related to school in either an official or unofficial way.

Blue had let Craig drive her home. Mistake number one. Then she had let him come up to her room. Mistake number two. The rest had been . . . awful. Well, most of it. First they had kissed, slowly and gently. But then his hands had started to roam all over her body. She still remembered the steel grip of his arms as Craig had pinned her down on the mattress. *You want it, baby. I know you want it.* She remembered hearing a high-pitched scream.

Thank God for Dylan. No one but she, Craig, and Dylan knew what had happened next. Dylan had burst into her room, grabbed Craig, and pulled him off her. Dylan had seen the fear in Blue's eyes . . . and flown into a rage. Craig had needed six stitches, and Blue had spent an hour scrubbing the blood off the hardwood floor of her bedroom. She shook her head, tossing away the memories.

Blue left the window and flopped back in bed. She never wanted to be pinned down like that again. Not by Jason. Not by anyone. Jason's I-love-you had been no big deal. It had been nothing. Jason was an emotional person—and so was she, in her own way. Friends told friends the *L* word all the time. Jason had barely been conscious when he had said the words. He probably thought he was talking to his mom. Or his dog. He told the Kirks' yellow lab, Morrison, that he loved him all the time.

Yes, that was it. Jason had momentarily

7

confused Blue with his dog. Mistakes like that happened all the time.

"Thou shalt not kill," Natalie van Lenton said, staring at herself in her full-length mirror. "Even if thine sister *is* a two-faced, backstabbing laboratory specimen."

Natalie yanked a brush through her long dark hair. "However, thou *shalt* refuse ever to speak to her again." And if Mia ever needed a kidney, she was toast.

Natalie pulled the brush away from her head, tearing out a large chunk of tangled hair in the process. The physical pain felt good. Anything was better than the dull ache in her heart.

I will survive, Natalie told herself. "Don't neeeed you byyy my siiidde," she sang at the mirror.

Thank goodness for Gloria Gaynor. Her seventies hit "I Will Survive" had probably kept thousands of females from jumping off the Golden Gate Bridge (or whatever bridge happened to be geographically convenient) when their husbands/boyfriends/crushes had shunned them blatantly. In front of everyone they knew. In favor of their sister.

But even a full-on medley of disco tunes wasn't going to keep Natalie from feeling like the gum scraped off the bottom of someone's shoe.

Actually she felt worse than that. She felt like the toilet paper *attached* to the gum on the bottom of someone's shoe. And there was exactly one person responsible for that fact.

Well, two people. Matthew Chance had crushed her. Natalie had been in love with him. For weeks she had planned and plotted to make him her boyfriend. New clothes, new makeup, new attitude. Everything was supposed to have been different this time. . . .

When Natalie had been in love with Dylan O'Connor, she was too shy to let him know how she felt. How many times had she sat across a table from Dylan, wishing, wishing, wishing that she had the nerve to ask him for a date? But she'd kept her mouth clamped shut. And then he and Tanya had become an item . . . and Natalie had buried her feelings for him so deep that she knew they were gone forever.

Yes, things were supposed to have turned out differently with Matthew. Last night should have been the best night of her life. Natalie had gone to Matthew's party full of hope. A tear slid down her cheek. Last night seemed like a lifetime ago.

Natalie closed her eyes as the moment of her ruin played in her head. She was standing close to Matthew, overhearing him talk about how beautiful she was, how much he wanted to be with her . . . or so she had thought. And then Mia had been at her side. Matthew had approached—and asked Mia to dance.

The memory hurt as much as the moment itself had. Matthew had never wanted her. He had never even given her a second thought. Mia was the one who he had been talking about. Mia was the one he wanted to kiss . . . to hold. She hated them both.

And now Natalie was not only heartbroken, she was utterly humiliated. Everyone had seen Matthew and Mia dancing. And they all knew how Natalie felt about Matthew. Why had she opened her big mouth and told half the world she was in love with Matthew Chance? She never wanted to be seen in public again.

Natalie lobbed her brush across the room. Her hair was way past the point where simple grooming was going to bring it back from the graveyard. And the enormous zit that had formed on the tip of her nose was something she didn't even want to acknowledge. Of course, she couldn't *help* but acknowledge it, seeing as her hazel eyes (which were currently red and puffy from a night of sobbing) seemed to have finally found something to complement. Yep. The green in her eyes highlighted Natalie's huge red pimple like a neon sign.

Natalie shuffled (girls with broken hearts don't walk—they shuffle) across the room and pulled open her bedroom door. There was coffee downstairs. And if she was going to go to work at @café even half prepared to deal with the day ahead, Natalie needed at least two cups of java to jolt her out of the sleepless-night, brokenhearted stupor she was in.

Natalie paused at the top of the van Lentons' back stairway, which led directly to the kitchen. Downstairs, she heard the whir of the blender. Natalie could picture the scene in her mind. Mr. van Lenton would be sitting at the kitchen table, drinking a cup of black coffee and grunting as he read the business section of the *San Francisco Business Times*. And Mia would be standing at the kitchen counter, grinding strawberries for her morning frappé. And where a mother should be—flipping pancakes, or nagging someone to take out the trash, or filling glasses with orange juice—there would be the same empty, painful hole that had been there since Natalie was five.

As Natalie walked slowly down the stairs she wished (as she did every day of her life) that her mom was still alive. Maybe if she could put her head in her mother's lap and cry her eyes out over the fact that the guy she was in love with barely knew she was alive, Natalie wouldn't feel so alone. Or like such a failure.

"Good morning, hon," Mr. van Lenton said as Natalie walked into the kitchen. He gave her a perfunctory smile over the top of his newspaper.

"Morning," Mia said over the din of the blender.

"Good morning, *Dad*," Natalie said, throwing

her sister a glare that she hoped would melt the excess of makeup on her perfect face.

"Good morning, Mia. So lovely to see my big sister on this bright, sunny morning," Mia said.

Natalie chose to ignore her sister's mocking voice. "Do you want an egg white omelet?" she asked her father.

Natalie cooked healthy, low-cholesterol meals for her dad whenever she could. She lived in fear of her father keeling over and dying of a massive heart attack. She wouldn't have minded, however, if Mia clogged her arteries with saturated fat and egg yolks.

"I'd love an omelet, Nat," Mr. van Lenton responded. He looked up from his newspaper again. "Hey, what's wrong? You look awful."

Natalie shrugged. She wasn't overeager to explain to her dad that last night she had been dissed by the love of her life in front of half of Alta Vista High School. And she wasn't thrilled to discover that the dark circles under her eyes she had seen in the mirror hadn't been a figment of her imagination. She did, in fact, look as bad as she felt.

Mia turned off the blender. "A little blush can go a long way, Nat."

Natalie wanted to restrain herself. She really, really did. "Shut up!" she yelled.

Mia arched one eyebrow. "So much for sisterly advice."

"Girls, please." Mr. van Lenton was using his weary-dad voice.

"I don't *have* a sister," Natalie hissed. She walked to the refrigerator and pulled open the door as hard as she could. "I have an overgrown wart that's so mentally unstable, she can't feel good about herself unless she's going around stealing other people's guys."

So much for Natalie not letting her dad in on her humiliation. She obviously needed some kind of self-help book about how to learn to control her emotions.

Mia finished pouring her strawberry frappé into a tall glass. "Excuse me?"

Natalie grabbed a carton of eggs. "Don't pretend like you weren't crawling all over Matthew on the dance floor last night."

"Did you have some kind of psychotic breakdown when I wasn't looking?" Mia asked. "Maybe I should make you an appointment with Chippa."

Natalie rolled her eyes. Chippa was Dr. Chippa Reynolds, Mia's ever present psychiatrist. A few years ago Mia had developed a nasty case of anorexia nervosa and was hospitalized. Mia was fine now (more or less), but she was addicted to weekly sessions with the omniscient Chippa. And Mia's mission in life was to get everyone she knew into therapy so they could "evolve."

"Don't talk to me," Natalie snapped, cracking an egg against the side of the counter with about a hundred times more force than was necessary.

13

"Girls, it's nine o'clock in the morning," Mr. van Lenton said. "Now is not the time to put on the boxing gloves." He set down the newspaper and gave them a hopeful smile.

"I sincerely hope that you aren't mad at me because I danced with Matthew Chance," Mia said, ignoring Mr. van Lenton. "He *asked* me. . . . Besides, it's not like he's your boyfriend—you barely know him."

"I *do* know him," Natalie insisted. "He personally invited me to his party last night."

Mia took a dainty sip of her frappé. "I didn't know you had a crush on him, Nat. And FYI, Matthew gave most of San Francisco a personal invite to his bash."

"I *don't* have a crush on him." Natalie separated the egg so that just the white fell into a small glass bowl. "Not that it would matter if I did. He didn't even look in my direction once you put him under one of your wicked spells."

This was pathetic. Beyond pathetic. Natalie couldn't even believe the words that were coming out of her mouth. How had she sunk to this level? The only thing worse than being totally humiliated was to whine about it afterward. She grabbed another egg and prepared to crack it. If only Mia's head fit so easily into her hand.

Mia dumped the rest of her frappé into the sink. "Face facts, little sister. You never had a chance with Matthew to begin with."

Natalie stared at the egg she was holding.

There was no way she was going to finish making this omelet. She wasn't even going to have the cup of coffee she had been looking forward to.

Because Natalie had other plans. She was going to sprint upstairs to her room—and bawl her eyes out.

BACK　FORWARD　HOME　STOP

LINK:

Sam Asks Readers To
Spill the Beans
About Their Weirdest Dream Ever

Hey, you all. I'm doing some dream inventory (for personal reasons), and I want to know if I'm guaranteed a passport to the loony bin or if my dreams are more or less within the realm of normal. So let me hear about *your* wackiest nighttime rendezvous with your subconscious, and I'll post the results below. . . .

Kitty226: I dreamt that I was on a giant roller coaster, only there weren't any tracks, so we were just flying in these little cars. Then my seat belt came undone and I was about to fall out. As I went over the edge of the car I grabbed my boyfriend's arm so we could fall together. Does that mean I'm selfish? Or romantic?

Arniebats43: One word—Madonna.

SINCITY44: Dream? This was a nightmare. I was in the dentist's chair and all my teeth were falling out. The dentist was coming at my bare gums with a huge drill and I was, like, peein' in my pants. But then the dentist turned into my mom. You know how stuff like that happens in dreams? And my mom was telling me that my teeth were all coming out 'cause I didn't eat enough zucchini. I don't know what it means, but I'm definitely planning to get my teeth cleaned every six months like I'm supposed to.

Elliefunt555: Two words: *Brad* and *Pitt*.

Thanks, all . . . I'll be back with more on the subject of dreams.

Sam Bardin tried to ignore the extremely unpleasant sounds that were emanating from his Honda motorcycle. He really needed to get a new muffler. At least, he was relatively sure that the muffler was the problem. Sam wished (not for the first time) that he had taken the auto shop class that had been offered when he was a sophomore at Alta Vista. Now he was almost eighteen years old, and he barely even knew how to change a tire. He barely knew how to do *anything*.

Maybe he should enroll in some kind of vocational school or send away for a correspondence course. General Life Skills 101 would probably be something he could manage. . . .

Uh-oh! The pothole was close. Very close. Too close to possibly avoid. Sam closed his eyes as the Honda lurched over the gaping wound in the road. The motorcycle landed—hard—on the other side of the pothole.

"Ouch!" Eddie Bardin yelled from his precarious position on the back of Sam's bike. The two surfboards that Eddie was balancing across his lap dangled precariously over one side of the motorcycle.

TWO

"Sorry," Sam shouted as Eddie regained control of the boards.

This was exactly why he didn't like being responsible for the safety of others. What if the bike had spun totally out of control and crashed into a light post? Eddie's head (even with the helmet on) could have exploded. As long as Sam was the only one risking death or possible paralysis, he thought motorcycles were great. But he certainly didn't want his little brother's life on his hands—on the bike or anywhere else. Unfortunately Sam was basically the only person Eddie had to rely on these days.

Sam turned onto Blume Street. @café was halfway down the block, but as soon as he rounded the corner Sam could see the freshly painted sign that Dylan had hung outside to attract new customers. The street was almost entirely empty—Saturdays in the Haight district started late. Sam wouldn't even have been awake at this hour if he hadn't promised Eddie that he would take him surfing. Instead Sam would still be dreaming about . . . *Natalie.*

Sam cut the engine of the Honda and let the bike coast the final few yards to the café. "First stop," he called to his brother. "I want a large black coffee—and don't let Dylan charge you for it."

Eddie slid off the motorcycle. "You don't want to come in?" He pulled off the *Easy Rider* helmet he had picked up at a garage sale and shook out his shaggy dark hair.

18

Sam shrugged. "If I go inside, I'll get caught up in some conversation and lose my will to surf." He didn't add that it was possible Natalie was in the café—and he was sure that as soon as he saw her his face would turn a lovely shade of red.

Sam put down the kickstand of his motorcycle but remained sitting on the bike. The dream that had been interrupted by Eddie's insistent banging on the bedroom door still lingered. . . .

Matthew Chance's party was in full swing. All around Sam people were dancing and laughing. In the shadows of the backyard several couples were making out passionately.

Sam watched Natalie from across the lawn. Her head was thrown back in laughter, her dark hair shimmering in the moonlight. As Sam watched, Natalie walked slowly toward him.

His heart pounded. Sam couldn't tear his eyes away from Natalie's long legs. This was Natalie his friend . . . and more. She stopped in front of him. Sam pulled her close, and they began to kiss—

"Sam! Wake up!" Eddie snapped his fingers in front of Sam's face. "I just asked if you want anything to eat."

Sam blinked. Man, what a dream that had been. "Sorry, I guess I'm a little, uh, preoccupied."

Eddie looked concerned. "Are you thinking about Mom?"

Sam *had* been spending most of his free time

worrying about their mother. Since Sam and Eddie's father had been sent to prison a couple of months ago, Mrs. Bardin had plunged into a deep depression. But for once his parents' problems were the last thing on his mind.

"I've got a woman on my mind," Sam admitted. "But she's a lot younger than Mom, if you know what I mean."

Eddie laughed. Sam's fifteen-year-old brother cherished every macho, male-bonding tidbit that Sam threw his way. He gave Sam a light punch on the shoulder. "So? Do you want something or not?"

"Get me a doughnut." Sam settled himself more comfortably on the seat of his Honda.

As Eddie turned to go into the café Sam revved the engine of his motorcycle. He couldn't wait to get back on the road. Sam needed to go for a good, hard ride. And pray that he could fill his mind with something other than romantic thoughts about Natalie van Lenton.

Dylan O'Connor picked up his discarded T-shirt and rubbed the soft cotton against his forehead and chest. He was used to working fifteen-hour days, but he couldn't remember the last time he had sweated so much before ten o'-clock in the morning. Apparently moving heavy boxes and throwing out several hundred pounds worth of accumulated junk was better exercise than any personal trainer could offer.

But the backbreaking work had been well worth the effort. Now that this room was empty, Dylan could envision the kitchen that he had promised Natalie he would put into the café. Of course, buying an oven, a stove, cabinets, counters, and another refrigerator was going to put him in major debt. But the extra cost would eventually pay off. Dylan was sure of that.

When Dylan had used all of his college savings to buy @café from Maxwell Lester, his former boss, he hadn't thought very far into the future. One day Maxwell had announced that he was retiring and moving to Portland, Oregon. The next day Dylan had decided that college could wait a few years. Now the café was in more or less full working order, and Spill the Beans, the web site that the whole staff of @café (plus Sam) contributed to, was up and running.

Looking at this empty room, which until this morning had been an unofficial dump for every unwanted paper cup, broken-down coffeemaker, and legless table that had crossed @café's threshold, Dylan felt the true pride of ownership. With Natalie's gourmet expertise Dylan was going to bring something new to the café—food.

Natalie. How many times had her name run through his head in the last, say, thirty seconds? Three, at least. More important, how many times had he thought of her since last night?

Last night had been . . . what? Unique, definitely. Incredible? Well, yes. At least, according to Dylan it had been incredible. He felt like getting on the ground and worshiping at the feet of Matthew Chance. Okay, *part* of him felt like getting Matthew alone in a dark alley and punching him until he lost consciousness. But Matthew was the person Dylan had to thank for his revelation about his own true feelings for Natalie.

Dylan sat down on the stepladder he had been using to reach the cobwebs attached to the ceiling. Last night still felt like a dream. For the last few weeks Natalie had been a woman with a one-track mind. She had been determined to make Matthew Chance, pretty boy extraordinaire, fall in love with her. She had changed the way she dressed, her makeup, even her hair in order to get Matthew's undivided attention.

In the process Dylan had seen good old dependable Natalie in a whole new light. A bright, flashing neon light. And then last night had happened. Natalie had shown up at Matthew Chance's party, planning to entice Matthew. But Matthew hadn't responded the way any sane individual would. He had ignored Natalie and asked Mia to dance. Enter Dylan.

In the one gallant move of his entire eighteen-year-old life, Dylan had stepped in and swept Natalie onto the dance floor. Even at that moment Dylan had been convinced that his motives came purely from a sense of big brotherly duty. But then he had felt her in his arms. For one song, and then another, and then another. The smell of her hair had been enough to keep him on the dance floor all night. Anything to keep her close.

Dylan had lain awake all night, obsessing over every detail of the evening. At six o'clock in the morning he had given up on the idea of sleep and had come into the café. And now he knew what he had to do. He had to tell Natalie how he was feeling.

Tanya Childes sat in a booth at @cafe and stared into the now lukewarm cup of mochaccino that was sitting in front of her and thought of Major Johnson's face. She was exhausted—she had stayed up most of the night, replaying her and Major's good-night kiss (okay, kisses, plural) over and over in her head.

He was . . . incredible. First there was the matter of his out-of-this-world good looks. Major Johnson was six feet and two inches of pure sex appeal. He had huge dark eyes, smooth chocolate brown skin, and a smile that said "kiss me" in about ten different languages.

Tanya could hold her own with Major in the looks department. She was five-eight, with a figure to rival Halle Berry's. And her dark skin had been described by certain members of the opposite sex as black velvet. Even Tanya had to admit that her bad hair days were few and far between. Her luxurious black curls looked good no matter where they happened to fall. But lack of sleep wasn't a great beauty enhancer. At the moment Tanya's brown eyes were puffy, and her hair seemed to be playing host to a squirrel's nest.

Tanya was supposed to start her morning shift in ten minutes, but waiting on bratty bow-head girls was the last thing she felt like doing. . . . She wished she were back in Major's battered Austin Healy convertible, heading down an open road.

Tanya sighed. There was nothing in the whole world—the whole Milky Way galaxy—that compared to meeting a gorgeous guy in the middle of the summer. Blending sun, hormones, and smooth soft skin was almost dangerous.

Tanya glanced up as Natalie sat down across from her. "So?" Natalie asked. "How did it go with Major?"

Tanya reached for the cup of fresh coffee that her best friend was holding. Natalie was light and sweet all the way. The coffee had so much sugar in it that Tanya felt as if she were sipping on a glazed doughnut. But swallowing saved her from talking—and she had no idea how to respond to Natalie's question.

Natalie reclaimed the coffee cup. "Give, Childes. I want to know everything."

When he kissed me, I felt like I had died and gone to endorphin heaven. When he dropped me off at my house, I was depressed the moment he was out of my sight. In short, he's an amazing specimen of what every male would be in an ideal world.

Tanya shrugged. "He said he would call me."

"Is it love?" Natalie asked.

Love. There were lots of four-letter words in the English language that Tanya considered taboo. And *love* definitely topped the list. "He's a cute guy," she responded. "But that's as far as it goes."

"Who knew that an afternoon excursion to see Sam's dad in prison would lead to a great romance?" Natalie mused.

Tanya grinned as she remembered her first encounter with Major. Thank goodness she had accompanied Sam during his heart-wrenching journey to the minimum security prison where his dad was incarcerated for tax evasion. And double thank goodness that Major had been there the very same day, working on an independent study project.

"I don't think it's going to be a great romance, as you put it," Tanya said. "Major informed me *umpteen* times that he's not looking for a relationship."

"At least he didn't humiliate you in front of sixty of his closest friends," Natalie said. She slumped so far down in the booth that a few loose strands of hair dipped into her coffee mug.

Tanya was immediately assaulted by an all too familiar sensation: guilt. There were a few details about Matthew's past that Tanya had neglected to

25

fill Natalie in on. Among those not so minor details was the fact that Tanya had fooled around with Matthew last year—and had been dumped by Dylan as a result. Tanya had *also* fooled around with him last weekend—long after she knew that Natalie's greatest wish in life was to make out with Matthew in the backseat of his Acura.

Tanya took a deep breath. "Matthew simply danced a few times with Mia. It doesn't mean anything."

Natalie yanked a paper napkin from the dispenser on the table and dabbed at her coffee-coated hair. "Don't patronize me, T." She wadded up the napkin in a very tight, very crumpled ball. "We both know the guy doesn't know I exist."

This was exactly the kind of moment that Tanya despised. Should she spare her best friend's feelings (in the short run) by telling a little white lie? Or should she be brutally honest, knowing that Natalie wasn't going to be happy until she put Matthew in the past? Besides, she had no idea whether or not Matthew would someday become interested in Natalie. The fact that he had spent several hours drooling over Mia didn't necessarily mean anything. Ticktock. Ticktock. Think, Tanya, think.

Natalie slurped her coffee. "Don't bother to lie," she said flatly.

"He's not worth your time," Tanya said, avoiding the question of whether to lie or not to lie altogether.

"I hate Mia." Natalie didn't even sound angry.

"You'll find someone who really deserves you," Tanya said. She lowered herself in the booth so that she could look Natalie in her eyes. "I promise."

Natalie shook her head. "There's something wrong with me, T."

Tanya snorted. "Come on, Nat. You're perfect."

"I'm doomed." She pushed her coffee to the edge of the table and leaned her head against the high red vinyl booth.

Tanya was instantly filled with self-loathing. True, Natalie and Matthew wouldn't have been meant for each other whether or not Tanya had fooled around with him. Still, if Natalie knew the truth . . .

"What's wrong?" Natalie asked suddenly. "You look like you're going to be sick."

Tanya attempted a lighthearted laugh. "I was just thinking about how we're going to chuckle about this when you're madly in love with a guy who's so cool that he makes Matthew Chance look like a toxic combination of Beavis and Butt-head."

Natalie smiled—her brave smile. "Maybe you're right . . . but I doubt it."

For the first time ever, Tanya was actually glad that her waitress shift was about to start. She couldn't stand Natalie's sadness. Furthermore, she couldn't stand herself. Tanya stood up. It would serve her right if Major never called. . . .

This Week *Chef Natalie* Presents a New Recipe:
Humble Pie à la Mode

Ingredients:

(1) Fantasy that you've convinced yourself will come true. Note: Such fantasies might have to do with getting that promotion, landing a guy/girl, or scoring the winning touchdown in the championship football game.

(2) Night (or morning or afternoon) that you've been looking forward to for your entire life.

(3) New wardrobe (complete with makeup and hair accessories) if appropriate.

(4) Large dash of stupidity (substitute with nerve or arrogance, if desired)

Directions:

Marinate fantasy for several days, weeks, or months. Stir in new wardrobe (if applicable) slowly. Parade the well-marinated fantasy in front of sixty or seventy of your closest friends/workmates/team-mates at the morning/noon/night you've been looking forward to your whole life. Turn up the heat in your own personal oven. Allow fantasy to come to a full-on boil. Wait to get burned. You now have Humble Pie. Go home and bury your humiliation in a pint of Ben & Jerry's ice cream. You now have Humble Pie à la Mode. Enjoy!

Jason Kirk was trying very hard to concentrate on reading the back of his box of Froot Loops. It was two o'-clock in the afternoon, and he had less than an hour to get to the café. He had never realized there was so much sugar in one bowl of cereal. Maybe he should switch to Grape-Nuts or Cheerios.

Jason picked up the box of Froot Loops and shook it. The box was still about half full. Maybe when it was empty, he would consult Blue about a new brand of breakfast food. Blue. That's exactly the place he hadn't wanted his mind to go. . . .

Blue. She was always beautiful, but last night he had felt like he was seeing her for the first time. The whole night had felt like a dream . . . especially when he had snuck into her house in the middle of the night. Jason still wasn't sure why he had gone over there.

He had told himself he was just looking for company. But as soon as he had seen her, framed by the dim light emanating from inside the house, he realized he wanted more. The urge to kiss her had almost been too much to bear.

THREE

But he hadn't just wanted to kiss her. He had wanted to tell her that he loved her. That he wanted to be with her forever. He had murmured the I-love-you part, but he wasn't even sure she had heard. Hopefully not. Because in the glaring light of day he realized he had been suffering from temporary insanity. Blue had told him a thousand times, in a thousand ways, that she didn't consider him boyfriend material. She didn't deserve to have his feelings forced onto her . . . no matter how hard it was to keep them inside now that he knew the truth.

"Hey, bro, have you found the secret decoder ring at the bottom of the box yet?" Jason jumped. Malcolm Kirk, his twenty-one-year-old brother, was standing in the doorway of the Kirks' kitchen.

Jason set down the Froot Loops on the pine breakfast table and glanced suspiciously at his brother. "What are you doing here?"

Malcolm grinned. "Is that any way to greet the prodigal son?"

Jason laughed. He couldn't help himself. Malcolm was the one member of the Kirk clan who seemed not to have inherited one family trait. Mr. and Mrs. Kirk, as well as Jason and his fourteen-year-old sister, Rachel, were thin and wiry. They all had brown hair and blue eyes. But they didn't just resemble one another physically. They all tended to be neurotic (each in his or her own way) and pessimistic. Cynicism was their modus operandi.

But Malcolm defied all of that. He was six feet tall, with a head of thick blond (white blond) hair and the body of an ice hockey goalie. Malcolm *always* smiled, and he didn't even seem to know that the word *stress* existed in the English language. Malcolm's beat-up orange VW Bug was covered with several dozen bumper stickers he had collected over the years. They all delivered more or less the same message: If it ain't fun, don't do it.

"Shouldn't you be at a party somewhere?" Jason asked. "Or surfing? Or making out with Candy?"

Candy Henson was Malcolm's latest true love. How his brother could take a girl with the name Candy seriously was a mystery to Jason. Then again, most things about Malcolm were a mystery.

Malcolm walked across the all-white kitchen and plopped into the wicker chair across from Jason's. "Candy and I are history, bro."

"Was she too sweet for you?" It was a stupid joke, but Jason couldn't resist.

"Ha, ha." Malcolm lifted the box of Froot Loops to his mouth and let a handful of cereal fall into it. For a few moments he crunched loudly. "Actually Candy met a surfer named Seagull and decided to move to Hawaii with him."

Jason pushed away his empty bowl. "Does this fact bother you?" he asked.

Malcolm shrugged. "A girl has to do what a girl has to do, man."

Jason absorbed this bit of information. He was constantly amazed that his brother's carefree persona wasn't just a veneer. The guy truly didn't let anything

31

bother him. He probably gave Candy a big kiss on the lips and slapped Seagull a high five as the new couple headed off for the kinder waters of Hawaii.

"You still haven't said why you're here," Jason said finally.

The tiniest glimmer of concern flickered in Malcolm's hazel eyes. "I'm a little short on rent. It's almost two weeks late, and my housemates are threatening to throw my stuff into the street."

Okay, so maybe Jason and Malcolm had *one* thing in common. Neither brother handled anything resembling responsibility with great aplomb. Malcolm had attempted college. He had managed to squeak into UC Berkeley, then attended for exactly one and a half semesters.

One rainy March night Malcolm had dropped by the house to inform Mr. and Mrs. Kirk that he was dropping out of school, moving out of his dorm, and embarking on a journey to find himself. The journey had taken him as far as a four-bedroom apartment in the Haight that he shared with two guys and a girl.

"How much are you hitting Dad up for?" Jason asked. By now he was familiar with this routine. Malcolm's all-time record for holding a job had been seven weeks.

Malcolm cracked his knuckles. "Correction, J.J. I'm hitting up *Mom*."

Jason sighed. While he couldn't care less if Malcolm spent the rest of his life making burritos, selling tourists small plastic replicas of the Golden

Gate Bridge, or posing nude for art classes, his parents were a little more demanding. Every time Malcolm came home to panhandle, tensions mounted.

"Don't look so down," Malcolm said. "I'll deal with Mom and Dad just like I always do."

Jason threw up his hands. "And I'll stay out of it. Just like always."

Malcolm reached into the Froot Loops box for another handful of cereal. "What's up in your life, little brother?"

"Nothing." Malcolm always asked the same question, and Jason always gave the same answer.

"No hot babes on the horizon?" Malcolm asked.

Jason felt the Froot Loops churning in his stomach. The subject of hot babes was one he wanted to avoid at all costs. He couldn't tell anyone about his feelings for Blue. It was too dangerous. "Nope."

Malcolm raised one eyebrow. "What's up with you and the lovely Blue?"

Danger! Danger! Malcolm seemed stupid, but he had an irritating habit of being incredibly perceptive. "Same as always," Jason said gruffly. "We're friends."

"You two are like Romeo and Juliet without all the kissing under the balcony," Malcolm commented. "You should get with the program and go for it."

Jason pushed back his chair. He had to get Blue out of his mind . . . otherwise, he would keep going over and over those words in his mind. *I love you. I love you. I love you.*

33

Jason wanted that memory to go away. He wanted to lock last night away and forget about Blue's slinky sundress and shiny brown hair. Blue was his lifeline. If Jason messed up their friendship by laying on Blue the fact that he'd been struck dumb by the sight of her perfect little nose and slender waist, he would have nothing.

Blue had made it clear from the beginning of their friendship that she didn't believe in romance, he reminded himself for the tenth time since he had woken up. Jason wasn't going to challenge her. He wouldn't dare.

It was now almost four o'clock in the afternoon. Dylan had pondered pulling Natalie aside and declaring his undying love for her for over six hours now. And he wasn't any closer to actually coming out from behind the safe haven of the counter and doing it.

"I need a café au lait and an espresso," Natalie said. "Table two needs a serious attitude adjustment." The glamour girl from last night was gone. Natalie was wearing a pair of faded Levi's and a white Gap T-shirt. The apron around her waist was stained with coffee and chocolate. She looked beautiful.

"Sure thing," Dylan responded. He tried to start making the espresso and stare at Natalie at the same time.

Natalie took a step closer to the counter. "Thanks again for last night," she said quietly. "I wouldn't have made it out of that party alive without you."

Dylan decided to abandon the espresso maker and focus solely on Natalie. Table two could wait. "Sure, uh, no problem . . ."

Natalie nodded toward the two girls sitting at table two. "Hello, Dylan! Café au lait and an espresso, please."

Dylan gulped. Do it! Tell her that last night was . . . amazing. "About last night—"

"You're such a great guy," Natalie interrupted. "You're like my very own big brother, only without the bad stuff that comes with belonging to the same set of parents."

Dylan turned his attention back to the espresso maker. Maybe now wasn't such a great time to talk to Natalie. Dancing with him clearly hadn't been a life-altering experience for her. And this was one situation that needed to be approached delicately at best. There were so many factors to consider. For one, Natalie was his ex-girlfriend's best friend. Intrafriend dating didn't go over so well with girls. And there was the Great Pact. After he and Tanya had broken up, they had all sworn that they would never date anyone who existed within the circle of their group friendship again.

"Yeah, well, I do what I can," Dylan muttered. Since when had it taken so long to make one lousy espresso?

"I mean, I thought I would die when Matthew walked right past me and asked Mia to dance," Natalie said. "But I didn't. I even managed not to dream about him last night."

"That's great, Nat." Dylan finished the espresso. All he had to do was put together a quick café au lait and Natalie (and her babbling about Matthew) would be safely headed over to table two.

"Tanya keeps saying Matthew wasn't right for me in the first place," Natalie continued. "What do you think?"

Like he really needed to think about the answer to that question. "I think Tanya's right," Dylan said quickly. "Matthew has zero to offer."

Natalie leaned against the glass case that held a wide assortment of pastries. "I still want to kill Mia."

Dylan wasn't sure how to respond. Should he support her desire to kill her sister and win points for loyalty? Or should he point out that Mia had done Natalie a favor by diverting Matthew's attention and hope so that Natalie came to her senses?

"Yeah, well, you know how it is," he said finally. It was the best nonstatement he could come up with while pouring coffee into a giant mug.

Dylan placed the drink orders onto the tray Natalie held out to him and prayed for some kind of divine intervention. "Thanks for the talk, Dylan. I feel much better."

Dylan sank onto the stool that stood behind

the cash register. An analysis of Matthew Chance wasn't exactly the heart-to-heart he had been hoping for. But intimate conversation about *anything* was better than no intimate conversation at all.

Maybe by tonight . . . or tomorrow . . . Dylan would find the right words to tell Natalie how he felt.

"Out!" Blue ordered. She pointed at the three twelve-year-old (or thereabouts) boys who were sitting in the booth and jerked her thumb toward the door. It was five o'clock, less than two hours into her shift at the café.

"We're not doing anything!" one of them insisted. He had floppy red hair and a face dusted with freckles.

"That's the problem," Blue countered. "We're not running a playground here. Either buy something or leave."

Boy Number Two stuck out his tongue at Blue. "We don't have any money. How can we buy anything?"

Blue snapped her fingers. "Exactly my point."

The three boys looked at one another, then at Blue. One by one they slid out of the booth. "And don't come back!" Blue called to their retreating backs.

"Hey, Sergeant O'Connor, where do I sign up for boot camp?" Tanya asked. She was sitting at a nearby table, relaxing over a cup of coffee and the July issue of *In Style* magazine after the end of her shift.

"Don't say a word," Blue said. She knew she had been unnecessarily harsh, but she didn't care. Her mood had turned decidedly foul since she had come on duty.

Tanya lifted her mug as if she were offering Blue a toast. "My lips are sealed."

"Good. Keep it that way." Blue plunked her butt into the chair opposite Tanya's. She hated herself when she felt this way.

"Want to talk about it?" Tanya asked. She flipped her magazine shut and stared at Blue.

Blue shook her head. "No." Tanya was a great friend, but she wasn't the person Blue felt most comfortable confiding in. Blue usually spilled her guts to Jason. Unfortunately Jason was the problem. He had barely said a word to her since he had shown up for work.

True, she had decided this morning that she wasn't going to make a big deal out of last night when she saw Jason. She was going to act exactly as she did every other day. But she hadn't planned to *ignore* him.

"I just saw Jason head into the storeroom," Tanya commented.

Blue glanced toward the back of the café. The storeroom door was ajar. "So?"

Tanya rolled up her magazine and tapped Blue on the head with it. "I'm not a mind reader, but it doesn't take a psychic to realize you're mad at Jason."

Blue frowned. She wasn't mad, exactly. She was

confused and hurt . . . and okay, a tiny bit angry. "Who said anything about Jason?"

Tanya grinned. "You did. The look on your face just told me that my guess was right on target."

Blue rolled her eyes. "If you'll excuse me, I have some business to attend to."

"In the storeroom?" Tanya asked.

"As a matter of fact, yes." Blue stood up. "I have to, uh, check on the paper napkin supply."

"Whatever you say, Sarge." Tanya waved the rolled-up magazine as if it were a magic wand. "And your fairy godmother is sure that your current foul mood has nothing to do with Jason *or* the party last night."

Blue stomped across the café, ignoring the fact that a guy at table six was waving frantically for service. This was humiliating. She and Jason had been best friends for a long time without any interference from outside parties. Blue was *not* interested in Tanya (and who knew who else) speculating about some kind of imaginary fight she and Jason were having.

Blue paused outside the door to the storeroom. What exactly was she planning to say? *Why did you tell me you loved me, then tiptoe out of my bedroom at dawn? Why haven't you spoken to me for the past two hours?* Nothing seemed quite right.

Blue pushed open the door of the storeroom another inch and peered inside. Jason was perched on the stepladder, staring into space. "Hey," Blue said. She walked into the tiny room

39

and closed the door (most of the way) behind her.

Jason looked up. "Oh, hey, Blue . . . I was just, uh . . ."

"Hiding?" Blue guessed. She leaned against a shelf of coffee beans and fixed him with her most penetrating stare.

Jason ran both of his hands through his already touseled hair. He looked different from last night—more like the Jason she was used to. The coral necklace he had worn to identify himself as Shyhunk was gone. And last night he had been clean shaven—this afternoon there was the slight shadow of a beard covering his cheeks.

"I'm not hiding," Jason insisted. "I'm just . . ."

Blue waited for him to finish. The silence was awkward and laden with questions. She couldn't take it anymore. "Did I *do* something?" she demanded.

"No!" Jason popped up from the stepladder and began to pace back and forth across the storeroom. "I did. I mean, I hope you're not mad that I came over last night."

"Why should I be mad?" Blue asked. "You come over all the time."

Jason nodded. "True . . ." He looked down as if the answer to the meaning of life were written on the toes of his Converse high-tops. "I didn't say anything weird last night . . . or anything, did I?"

Actually her own shoes were pretty intriguing, also. How did manufacturers get patent leather to be so darn shiny? "Uh, no . . . nothing."

Jason looked up. "Good."

"Yeah, great." Blue bounced up and down on her toes, acutely aware that the awkwardness between herself and Jason hadn't diminished one iota.

Jason bit his lip. "I guess last night was pretty bizarre all the way around, huh?"

"Yeah." Bizarre was one word for it, anyway. "Well, I just came in here to get some, uh, paper napkins." She bent down and pulled a container of napkins that she had absolutely no use for out of a large cardboard box.

"So let's just forget last night," Jason said. "Everything about it?"

She wasn't sure if he was making a statement— or asking a question. Was it possible that Jason was as confused as she was? Blue glanced at his face. His eyes were practically begging her to end the conversation. "It's forgotten," she said.

Relief washed over Jason's face. He sank onto the stepladder. "Phew . . . I'm glad we got that taken care of."

Tears were *not* threatening to well up in her eyes. She had simply been staring at the paper napkin label for too many seconds without blinking. "Me too," Blue agreed quietly.

She just wished that she *felt* as relieved as Jason *looked*. In fact, she wished she felt anything but totally and completely horrible.

Car Talk
Dylan O'Connor's Advice on
Buying a New Used Car

The act of buying a car is a delicate balance of art and science. Here's a breakdown of the two. . . .

The Science:

Look under the hood. Even if you know less than nothing about the way an engine is put together, it is imperative that you pretend as if you do. Whoever is trying to sell you the car is going to be studying your face for signs of both ignorance and weakness. As you peer at different engine parts, grunt a lot. Then ask some prepared question about the valves, the pump, or the axle. You must kick the tires. I have no idea why, but I know the kicking motion is of utmost importance. It implies that you can glean some kind of feeling about the car as a whole.

This is the most important aspect of the science. Find a friend who knows something about cars and take him/her with you to look at the vehicle in question. Then make sure that he/she follows the steps above.

The Art:

Sit in the driver's seat. How does the car make you *feel?* Warm and fuzzy? Dorky? Macho? Make sure you can live with whatever feeling that is.

1. View the car from afar. Is that the truck/convertible/sedan that you'll enjoy looking for in a crowded parking lot after a movie? If not, move on.
2. Bring your girlfriend/boyfriend with you. If she/he says looking at you in the car makes her/him feel amorous, buy it on the spot!

"Remind me again why I'm here," Sam said to Dylan Saturday evening.

"To help me find a car," Dylan answered. He had left Jason and Blue in charge of the café so that he could take a look at some used cars.

Sam had given Dylan a ride to Bob's Best Buy Cars on the back of his Honda. Now they were standing in the middle of a giant lot, surrounded by cars suffering various degrees of wear and tear. Over their heads was the symbol of used car lots all across America—a long streamer of small, triangular plastic flags.

"You realize I know nothing about cars," Sam said. "Especially used ones."

"At least you *had* one," Dylan responded. Before his family had filed for bankruptcy, Sam had been the proud owner of a black BMW convertible.

"I still say you should get a motorcycle," Sam said. He gestured toward the row of old Harley-Davidson motorcycles that lined one side of the large parking lot. "Guys on bikes are babe magnets."

"I'm more concerned with having a way to lug around supplies, baked

43

goods, and coffeemakers," Dylan said, heading for a vintage station wagon, complete with wood side paneling.

Sam was still staring at the Harley-Davidson motorcycles. "I wonder how Natalie feels about guys on motorcycles," he said.

Dylan had opened the door of the station wagon and slid into the driver's seat. He stuck his head out the window. A small knot formed in his large intestine. "Why do *you* care?"

Sam leaned against the side of the station wagon. He shook his head. "Never mind . . . it's crazy."

Dylan got out of the car and slammed the door shut. He didn't like the direction this conversation was heading. "Tell me," he ordered.

Sam covered most of his face with his hands. "It's too stupid," he muttered. *"I'm* stupid."

Dylan shrugged. "Fine. Now come with me to look at that pickup truck." Dylan started walking toward a battered red Toyota pickup.

Sam fell into step beside him. "I'vebeenhaving-dreamsaboutNatalie," he said in one breath.

Dylan stopped. "Excuse me?" Man, he wished he had never gone down this path. If Sam had said what Dylan *thought* he had said, Dylan was going to be beyond upset.

"I've been having dreams about Natalie," Sam repeated, more slowly this time.

The small knot was now the size of a fist. "What kind of dreams?" Dylan asked. Maybe Sam was dreaming that he wished Natalie was his mother. Or maybe he secretly hated her, and in his dreams he was chasing her with a butcher knife.

Sam raised one eyebrow—his trademark. "What kind do you *think*?"

Dylan continued toward the red truck. How was he supposed to respond to this revelation? Saying "me too" didn't seem appropriate. "I see. . . ."

"And all day I thought about how I'd like to kiss her," Sam said. "I mean, she looked so vulnerable . . . and she's so sweet."

"And beautiful," Dylan couldn't help adding.

Sam stopped next to the pickup. "But I'm totally insane, right?" When he turned to Dylan, his brown eyes were serious. "I mean, I shouldn't try to start something up with Natalie . . . should I?"

Dylan shook his head vigorously. Forcing actual words out of his mouth wasn't even within the realm of possibility. Sam didn't seem to notice Dylan's silence.

"For one thing, we all made that stupid pact. . . ." His voice trailed off as he leaned his head into the driver's side window to inspect the truck's interior.

"Right," Dylan said, finding his voice. "We all agreed not to date each other. You and Nat were definitely in on that."

Sam pulled his head back out of the car. "Yeah . . . but that whole pact was because of you and Tanya breaking up." He started walking toward a Chevy minivan. "Why should Natalie and I suffer because you and T. screwed up?"

Dylan didn't care that they had moved on to the next vehicle before he had a chance to check out the last one. Buying a car was suddenly very low on his list of priorities. "Pact or no pact, the idea of you and Natalie together doesn't make much sense."

Sam executed another eyebrow raise. "Why not?"

Dylan opened the passenger door of the Chevy and slid into the minivan. He needed a few seconds to think before he answered Sam's question. He wasn't about to tell him that the reason Sam and Natalie didn't make sense was because Dylan thought *he* and Natalie would be perfect together.

On the other side of the van Sam got into the driver's seat. "Come on, Dylan. Why not?"

"Because . . . Natalie is totally into Matthew Chance." Dylan flipped down the visor attached to the windshield so that he could look at something besides Sam's face.

Sam snorted. "Give me a break. Pretty boy isn't even a factor. Natalie will forget about him in a few days."

Dylan agreed. Natalie didn't care about Matthew as a person. As soon as she got over the sting of rejection he would be old news. Dylan needed another reason. A good one. "You never stick with one girl for more than a month or two. I don't want to see Natalie's heart broken."

Sam rested his hands on the minivan's giant steering wheel. "What if I decided that I wanted a real relationship? One that was going to last?"

About a gallon of coffee was churning danger-ously in Dylan's stomach. Tell him, Dylan ordered himself. Explain the real reason why you don't want him to go out with Natalie.

But he couldn't. Dylan certainly didn't want to pit himself against Sam, especially now, when Sam needed him most. Besides, Sam had never been serious about a girl in his life. This Natalie phase would probably pass by the time they got back to the café.

"Just don't do anything rash," Dylan said fi-nally. "The last thing we need around the café is more tension."

Sam nodded. "Like I said, it's a crazy idea."

Dylan started breathing again. Apparently Sam was already backing off the idea. "Right. Crazy."

A man wearing a brown suit and a cowboy hat with Bob's Best Buy written across it appeared at Sam's window. "Hey, boys. Can I help you find a car?"

So. The conversation was over, at least for now. And hopefully forever.

Work was good for the soul. Yeah, right. People had streamed in and out of @café from three o'clock to ten o'clock—but not one of those people had been Matthew Chance, telling her that he had made a horrible mistake when he asked Mia, instead of her, to dance last night.

47

Natalie concentrated on pedaling her new bike (the one she spent an outrageous amount of money on in order to have an excuse to visit Matthew while he was working at Freddie's Bikes) up the hill to her house. And as soon as she got inside the house she planned to run upstairs and retreat to her bedroom. She should be able to kill a good few hours listening to Alanis Morissette and crying her eyes out.

Natalie jumped off her bike in front of the van Lentons' three-story town house. What were the chances that Mia wasn't home? Probably a hundred to one. Mia had an uncanny ability to stick herself in Natalie's face at exactly the moments when Natalie least felt like seeing her.

Natalie wheeled her bike up the front path, wishing she was anyone but herself. Other girls met a cute guy, fell in love, and lived happily ever after. At least that's what happened in all the romance novels. But not Natalie. Oh, no. She had to crush out on a guy who wanted to stick his tongue down her dear sister's throat. And she was blessed (ha, ha) with a sister who was more than happy to oblige him.

Natalie stopped midstep. Her new bike banged against her leg. She was vaguely aware that she might have just sustained a bruise. But any injury seemed insignificant. Because Matthew Chance's superfancy, superexpensive bicycle was lying on the van Lentons' front porch.

Deep breath. Two deep breaths. No good.

Natalie was still hyperventilating. She had to think this through. Matthew was here. That was definitely his bike. So what did this mean?

Option A: Matthew was here to tell Natalie that he had been suffering from temporary insanity last night and he had been secretly in love with her for months.

Option B: Mia had called Matthew and lured him over. Now they were making out on the leather sofa in the den.

Either way Natalie had to go inside. She had a decent amount of willpower, but nothing was going to keep her from finding out exactly why Matthew Chance's bicycle was decorating her front porch.

Natalie dropped her own bike in the grass at the bottom of the porch stairs. She ran her hands over her ponytail, hoping she looked halfway decent.

Please let him be here to see me, Natalie prayed as she walked up the steps. Please let Matthew thrust a dozen roses into my arms the second I blow through the door. Please, please, please.

She opened the door. And heard voices in the den. Okay, so far not so bad. Clearly Matthew and Mia weren't making out. Kissing was done in silence, and Natalie heard the definite low murmur of Matthew's voice.

Natalie shut the front door oh so softly behind her. The element of surprise never hurt anyone.

She tiptoed to the side of the open door of the den and stood as still as she could, considering the fact that her knees were shaking.

"How about Wednesday night?" Matthew said (to Mia, Natalie presumed). Natalie swallowed. This didn't sound good.

"I have a shoot," Mia answered. Natalie swallowed again. At least she tried to. Her mouth was suddenly so dry that her tongue was sticking to the roof of her mouth.

Natalie wished that instead of having a modeling shoot (where she got paid an insane amount of money to smile and bare her cleavage), Mia was scheduled to be shot. A firing squad would solve all of Natalie's problems in a few split seconds.

"Thursday, then." Matthew's low, husky voice sent shivers down Natalie's spine. She crept closer to the den's entrance and peered inside.

Matthew and Mia were sitting on the van Lentons' black leather couch, so close to each other that their knees were touching. "I can't," Mia said. "I have a date."

Matthew moved even closer to Mia, if that was possible. "Saturday?" he asked.

Mia laughed. At least an objective person would have called it a laugh. Natalie thought the sound was something between a cackle and a banshee squeal. "Maybe. I'll get back to you."

Matthew grinned. "Victory!"

Mia stood up. "You should get out of here before . . ."

"Before what?" Matthew asked. He sounded reluctant to leave Mia's feline presence.

Natalie backed away from the door. She was amazed that her legs would actually move, considering the fact that her entire body was numb. Last night's humiliation hadn't been enough. Mia had apparently felt compelled to ask Matthew to come over as a way to drive the corkscrew deeper into Natalie's heart.

And now Natalie had to get out of this house. Immediately if not sooner.

Tanya Reveals How *Not* to Get Your Man

How many of you all have convinced yourself over a pint of ice cream and your hundredth viewing of *Sleepless in Seattle* that it really *is* okay for you to call that guy you've been lusting after all semester? So you glide to the phone and dial his number (which you memorized two weeks ago just in case). And Mr. Wonderful actually answers the phone! All right, now we're getting somewhere. So you two have this really awful, awkward conversation, during which time you mention over and over again how much you'd like to see him race his dirt bike. "Want to come to my race on Saturday?" he finally asks you. Your heart soars. He likes you! This is it. He is The One.

So you go to the race on Saturday. He wins, naturally, and you feel that special glow. After all, behind every good man there's a great woman. During the brouhaha after the race your guy is busy high-fiving his buds. But that's okay. You stick around until he finally notices you standing on the sidelines. He walks over to you. Your heart pounds. Then before he has a chance to tell you thanks-for-coming and walk away, you ask him out for pizza.

He accepts! Bring in the angels—this is truly a religious experience. After pizza you get real close to him. He kisses you . . . it's bliss. The two of you start to go out, which consists of you calling him and him blowing you off fifty percent of the time. It's a miserable way to live, but you don't care.

Four months later your guy falls head over heels for a cold, aloof girl who wouldn't call a guy if her life depended on it. Voilà! She has your dude, and you're dissed big time.

The lesson? *Never* call a guy if you want him to take you seriously.

"I didn't know you guys were going out," Gina Gold said to Blue and Jason. She was hanging on the arm of her boyfriend, Eric Mialta.

Blue and Jason were sitting at a small table in their favorite Japanese restaurant, Dojo's. After their shift at the café they had decided to go out and celebrate the fact that they had both come through the other end of their "blind dates" unscathed. Unfortunately they had been spotted by Alta Vista's most cloying couple.

Eric gave Jason a light punch on the arm. "I always knew you guys would get together."

"We're not going out!" Jason said. Had that been a shriek? "We're just friends."

Gina gave Blue one of those condescending smiles that Jason often saw girls with boyfriends give to girls *without* boyfriends. "Well, you sure do look cozy," she said.

"Enjoy your meal," Blue responded. She was the master of the quick and easy brush-off.

"Don't do anything I wouldn't do," Eric said to Jason.

Jason watched the pair make their way toward the other side of

FIVE

the restaurant. Exhibit A as to why he knew relationships were a bad, bad idea.

Jason lifted his cup of hot green tea. "Here's to never going on another blind date," he said to Blue.

Blue lifted her cup. "I'll definitely drink to that."

Jason was glad that whatever weirdness had existed between him and Blue this afternoon had evaporated. He had successfully shoved every nonplatonic impulse down deep, where it couldn't threaten his valuable friendship.

Their personal dynamic (as Dr. Grady, his shrink, would call it) had been a little strained all afternoon. Blue had answered most of his questions with monosyllables. But once Dylan was gone, the atmosphere had lightened up a little. And finally Blue had laughed. Jason's private little world was back in sync.

"Can I level with you?" Blue asked after a few moments of companionable silence.

Jason set down his tea. "Sure . . . of course."

"I felt *really* uncomfortable after last night. I mean, getting set up on a date with each other and then spending the night . . . you know." Blue brushed her light brown hair over one shoulder. She seemed ultrafidgety.

"Yeah . . ." Jason wasn't sure what to say. Hadn't they covered this territory earlier?

"Anyway, I thought . . . I mean, I didn't *think* it, I just sort of . . ." Blue's voice trailed off. She took another sip of her tea.

"What?" Jason asked. Now he knew how Dr.

Grady felt when Jason refused to spit out whatever he was trying to say.

Blue giggled. Yes, a real giggle. The girl was losing it. "I just sort of had this totally insane idea that you were . . . *interested* in me."

"Uh-huh . . ." Jason was at a total loss for words. Blue had, like, seen into his brain and scoured out each and every one of his impure thoughts.

"But now that we've cleared up the fact that neither of us has any interest whatsoever in being anything but friends—best friends—I feel *much* better."

"Good." Jason hoped that he had managed to keep his sigh of relief from taking on any outward form.

Thank goodness he hadn't followed Malcolm's advice to "go for it." If he had let on to Blue that their so-called date had been anything more than a hilarious joke, she probably would have given him a nice, flat slap in the face.

A waitress appeared at the side of their table. She turned to Jason. "Have you and your girlfriend decided what you want?" she asked.

"She's not my girlfriend," Jason said quickly. Was there some kind of conspiracy going on here?

The waitress smiled. "Too bad for you."

Jason glanced at Blue, who had picked up her menu. She seemed intent on perusing the list of each and every item that Dojo's offered. Jeez! As long as Blue was the one who insisted on keeping their friendship at a level that didn't include anything beyond an occasional high five, Jason thought the least she could do was bail him out of an awkward situation.

Finally Blue looked up from her menu. "I'm a lesbian," she said to the waitress. "So I'm sure you can understand that any kind of romantic entanglement between myself and this gentleman is out of the question."

The waitress looked from Blue to Jason and back to Blue in clear confusion. Jason tried not to laugh. "Well, do you two want to, uh, order?" the waitress asked.

Blue nodded. "Yes. We know exactly what we want."

Jason leaned back in his chair. Blue always knew exactly what she wanted. Jason just wished that he did. . . .

Tanya lifted the can of Pringles lites she had just inhaled and tipped it upside down so that the crumbs fell into her mouth. She glanced at the kitchen clock as she munched. Great. It was now ten twenty-five. She had killed exactly twenty-five minutes by eating herself into a junk food stupor.

It's been less than twenty-four hours, Tanya reminded herself. No guy with any pride whatsoever called a girl so soon after their first date. If the house weren't so quiet, she wouldn't even be thinking about Major. Why was it that parents always chose to go out on the town on the very night that their children actually wanted to have them around?

Tanya glanced around the kitchen, looking for something to do. Even loading the dishwasher sounded thrilling at this point. Since getting home from @café, she had rearranged the furniture in her room, given herself a facial, and watched back-to-back episodes of *Singled Out* on MTV.

Unfortunately the kitchen was spotless. Mrs. Childes was a textbook neat freak. The black-and-white tile floor was freshly mopped, and the white Formica counters looked as though they were permanently coated with Fantastik. Tanya glared at the black Princess telephone attached to the wall. *Ring. Ring. Ring.*

Tanya closed her eyes and focused all her mental energy on willing the phone to make some kind of noise. One second passed. Two seconds. Her eyes popped open.

A sound! Tanya dove for the phone. "Hello," she said breathlessly. Pause. "Hello?"

Darn. No one was there. Just the droning sound of the dial tone. Maybe she had come down with some rare neurological disorder that made her imagine she was hearing phones ring. Or maybe she was just going insane.

Tanya jumped. There was the sound again! And again. She wasn't going crazy—she had heard the doorbell. Her heart pounded. Was it possible? Could Major already miss her so much that he had felt compelled to drop by at ten-thirty on a Saturday night?

Tanya ran her hands through her curly black hair and walked slowly down the hall that led from the kitchen to the front door. Hello, Major. I was just in the middle of researching a cure for cancer. Hello, Major. You caught me in the middle of my second read-through of *War and Peace*. She took a deep breath and pulled open the door.

"Dingdong. It's the Avon lady." Natalie was standing on the front porch. But she wasn't alone. She was accompanied by a duffel bag so big that Tanya guessed Natalie's entire bedroom set could fit inside.

Okay, so it wasn't Major. But that was fine. Really. Tanya was happy to see her best friend standing on her porch. More than happy. She was absolutely, totally overjoyed. At least seeing Natalie was better than messing up bowls and plates just so she could put them into the dishwasher.

"Hey, Nat." Tanya glanced down at the duffel bag. "Are you planning a trip around the world that I didn't know about?"

Natalie grinned. Or grimaced—there was a fine line between the two. "I'm moving in," she announced.

Tanya took a step backward. Natalie wasn't known for making rash, improbable statements. That was Tanya's department. "Did I miss something?" Tanya asked.

Natalie grabbed one end of the duffel bag and dragged it into the foyer. "I hate my sister," she said. "I can't stand to look at her self-satisfied, backstabbing face one more time."

"Uh-huh." Tanya shut the front door behind Natalie. She noticed for the first time that Natalie's face was bright red and she seemed to be covered in a sheen of sweat. "Did you sprint over here or what?"

Natalie lifted up her T-shirt and used the bottom of it to wipe her forehead. "I rode my bike with the duffel on my lap."

Tanya raised her eyebrows. Natalie was obviously suffering from some kind of breakdown. "Well, that was very . . . athletic of you."

"Can I stay?" Natalie smiled hopefully. But her hazel eyes were decidedly puffy and red rimmed.

"For as long as you want," Tanya assured her.

"Good. We can hang around and discuss various ways to exact revenge upon my evil sister."

Tanya nodded, but the knots that had been in her stomach as she waited for some word from Major had suddenly spread to her neck and shoulders as well. If Natalie found out the truth about who had *really* betrayed her, Tanya could bet on losing her best friend in the world.

Blue kicked off her forest green Birkenstock sandals and propped her feet up on the ivory-colored ottoman that sat in the middle of the Kirks' small den. "This is *much* better than the arcade at the mall," she said to Jason.

Jason nodded. "We should have come here in the first place." He picked out a videocassette from the shelf underneath the Kirks' thirty-inch TV and popped it into the VCR. "Now, just sit back and relax. We've got four episodes of *The Larry Sanders Show* to watch."

"Fire it up." Blue picked up the mug of herbal tea that sat on the antique coffee table at her side.

Jason was right. Going out on the town in order to celebrate the end of their respective careers as "daters" had been a terrible idea. They hadn't been able to walk one lousy block without some well-meaning acquaintance commenting on what a cute couple they were. Blue had run into more people she knew in the last five hours than she had during the whole month of June.

Finally she hadn't been able to take it anymore. And neither had Jason. They had abandoned their plan to have a Ms. Pac-Man war at the arcade and retreated to the safety of the Kirks' house. This was one place where they could be sure they would be left in peace. Mr. and Mrs. Kirk were out for the evening, and Rachel, Jason's fourteen-year-old sister, was spending the night at a friend's house.

Jason grabbed the VCR's remote control and plopped down next to Blue on the sofa. He pulled off his Converse sneakers and nudged Blue's feet to one side of the ottoman to make room for his own. "I can't believe how annoying every single person we know is," he commented.

Blue nodded. "You'd think we were living in the 1950s. The concept of a platonic relationship is enough to send people over the edge."

"Well, that's their problem—not ours." Jason pressed the play button on the remote. Gary Shandling's face (which was funny in and of itself) popped up on the television screen.

"You said it, brother."

"Hallelujah!" Jason turned up the volume on the TV and switched off the halogen floor lamp at his side.

Blue was glad for the darkness. This entire day had been overwhelming. In the first light of morning she had thought that maybe, possibly, she and Jason would . . . what? And then at the café she had been angry because he was ignoring her. She had spent the afternoon mellowing out and the evening working herself up again. A lot of mental energy had been poured into the utterly ridiculous fallout from her botched date. For absolutely no good reason.

Blue was sure that the tiny, nagging pang she had felt tonight every time Jason had corrected someone about the status of their relationship was caused by nothing but an emotional hangover. Now that everything was resolved, she could relax.

Beside her Jason was laughing about something Hank, Larry's misguided sidekick, had said. At least she thought it was Jason. She hadn't realized that he giggled at such a high, soprano pitch.

"It's not *that* funny," Jason said to her now.

Blue turned to him. "What?"

Jason pushed the mute button. "Weren't you laughing hysterically just now?"

"No . . ." Acting on instinct, Blue whipped her head toward the double wooden doors that separated the den from the rest of the Kirks' house.

There were two sets of eyes peering into the dark room. One set belonged to Rachel Kirk, the other to her best friend, Chelsea Sutton. "Blue and Jason, sittin' in a tree," Rachel sang.

"*K-i-s-s-i-n-g* . . . ," Chelsea continued.

"First comes love, then comes marriage, then comes—" Rachel's high-pitched voice was cut off by a large throw pillow that had been lobbed directly at her head. "Hey!" she shrieked.

"Aren't you supposed to be at Chelsea's house?" Jason demanded.

Rachel shrugged. "We got bored there." Blue was struck by the resemblance between Jason and his sister. Rachel had the same sharply defined cheekbones and straight brown hair that Jason did.

"Are we *bothering* you?" Chelsea asked. She was one of those overly developed fourteen-year-old girls who tried to hide their growing breasts by wearing T-shirts that would be roomy on a football player.

"Get out!" Jason yelled. He threw another pillow in Rachel's general direction.

Rachel giggled. "Come on, Chelsea," she said. "Blue and Jason want to be *alone*."

Blue watched the girls as they darted away from the door and toward the kitchen. She felt so uncomfortable that she thought she might be breaking out in hives.

Jason turned the light back on. "Sorry about that," he said quietly.

Blue set her now cold tea back on the table. "I've always been glad I don't have a little sister— now I know why."

Jason nodded. "I don't understand why everyone

62

can't worry about their own lives and leave ours alone."

"It's like they've all been lobotomized at birth," Blue said. "Every single person we know is missing exactly one half of their brain."

"I mean, the idea of us as boyfriend and girl-friend is so *completely* insane. . . . You'd think that even my little sister could see that."

Blue took the remote control from Jason's hand and turned the sound back on. "Yeah . . . you'd think so."

Blue stared at the TV set, wishing she were any-where but on this particular sofa. Jason acted as if being linked to her was akin to some nasty disease. She understood being a little uncomfortable, but did he have to be so . . . outraged? Sure, she didn't want anyone thinking Jason was her boyfriend. But the fact that he was so totally put out by the entire thing was . . . what? Something. Something bad.

Jason gave her a light punch on the shoulder. "As long as we know the truth, huh?"

"Yeah. Right. I couldn't agree more." She leaned her head against the back of the sofa and closed her eyes.

K-i-s-s-i-n-g. K-i-s-s-i-n-g. The stupid song played over and over in her mind. Blue sighed. At the moment she wished she had never learned how to spell.

BACK   FORWARD   HOME   STOP

LINK:

Blue's Sound Bytes:
Sara Jane O'Connor
on the Meaning of *Friendship*

I know all you Internet surfers like to ignore heavy, existential discussion topics. But this week I simply don't have anything to offer about the *true* killer of JFK or the downing of TWA Flight 800. Therefore I'm going to file away all my pet conspiracy theories and talk about friendship.

We all gather friends in a somewhat arbitrary manner. The girl who sits next to you in homeroom may be a total idiot, but hey, she invited you to her older brother's party. Voilà! You've found a friend for life. Remember that chemistry lab partner who wouldn't quit asking if you wanted to go see Howard Stern's *Private Parts*? Now he's your male-bonding soul mate. But there's more to a real friend than just someone to hang out with on a Saturday night.

Once the label—*friend*—has been attached, what exactly do we expect? Aha! Now we have come to the existential part of our debate. For starters, we want our friend to be happy every time he/she is lucky enough to gaze upon our face. And just smiling and saying "hey" isn't enough. The friend must engage in pleasant banter, which hopefully includes a few private jokes that make everyone else feel left out.

Furthermore, the friend must actively seek out our companionship: phone calls, E-mails, coded beeper messages, etc. *Anything* to let us know our company is in high demand. If the friends in question aren't fifty-fifty in the seeking-out part of the arrangement, then a serious rift is afoot.

Now look at yourself in the mirror and ask yourself if you're really being a friend.

Sam pulled up in front of @café and cut the engine of his motorcycle. It was eleven o'clock in the morning, but Sam already felt as if he had put in a whole day. What had happened to nice long Sundays in bed with a good book?

Dumb question. He knew what had happened. His dad was a convict, and his mom had turned into a neurotic recluse. Eddie had knocked on Sam's door at nine o'clock, begging to be taken from the House of Gloom.

So Sam had dropped off his little brother at @café and taken Dylan back to Bob's Best Buy, where Dylan had surprised them both by investing twenty-five-hundred dollars in a bright yellow 1972 Cutlass Oldsmobile convertible.

Dylan honked the horn of his "new" car as he pulled into the space behind Sam's. "We're home," he called. "And I've got wheels . . . talk about a great day."

Sam jumped off his bike. "This café is like home these days," he said, walking toward the Cutlass to inspect the body of the car one more time. "Except for sleeping and an occasional afternoon of trying to talk my mom out of her depression, I feel like I'm never at

the houseboat—and I don't even work here."

Dylan honked the horn again. "Where are those guys?" he asked. "I want everyone to come outside and praise my car."

As soon as the words were out of Dylan's mouth Natalie suddenly rushed out of the café.

"Check it out, Nat!" Dylan called. "Is this a car, or is this a *car*?"

Natalie didn't even glance in Dylan's direction. She stopped in front of Sam and put her hands on his shoulders. "I'm so sorry, Sam. I—"

Sam repressed his desire to stand still and enjoy the feel of Natalie's hands. Instead he took a step backward and studied her flushed face. "What happened?"

"There's an article in the newspaper about your dad. . . ." She looked as if she were about to start crying. "Eddie saw me reading it—"

"Oh, no . . ." Eddie's mental state was fragile at best. The last thing he needed was to see his dad's lurid story printed in black-and-white—again.

"If I had known . . . I mean, I just assumed that you told Eddie—"

Sam's heart sank. "Told Eddie what?"

But Sam didn't need to hear the answer to his question. Eddie had appeared at the door of the café, his face stormy. "How could you go see him and not tell me?" Eddie yelled.

Natalie gave Sam one more apologetic glance, then melted out of the line of fire. "Calm down," Sam said.

At the moment Eddie resembled Mount Saint Helens just before a major blowup. His chest was heaving, and his skin was blotchy.

"I mentioned your visit when he was reading the article," Natalie said softly.

"Why didn't you take me with you?" Eddie demanded. "Why?" He was yelling so loudly that several people walking by had stopped to watch the spectacle.

Sam put his hand around Eddie's neck and steered him toward the side of the café. "Let's talk out back—where our family dispute won't become a neighborhood spectator sport."

Eddie clamped his mouth shut. As they walked through the alley that led to the back of @café Sam noticed his little brother's jaw twitching uncontrollably. When they reached the rear of the café, Sam grabbed two milk crates.

"Sit," he ordered.

Eddie paced back and forth, waving his fists in the air. "You can't tell me what to do! You're not my father!"

Sam shrugged. "Fine. Stand." He sat down on one of the crates and stretched his legs out in front of him.

Eddie paused. He seemed confused by Sam's nonconfrontational manner. "Why didn't you take me with you?"

"If you would shut up for two seconds, I'd explain." Sam crossed his arms in front of his chest and waited to see if Eddie was going to yell some more.

His brother sank onto the other crate. "Start talking."

"Mom hasn't been doing that great . . . ," Sam began.

Eddie bounced off the crate again. "News flash! I'm the one who's been at home twenty-four /seven, making sure she doesn't blow out her brains."

Sam stared at his brother, absorbing what he had just said. He knew Eddie had been aware that their mom was giving a whole new meaning to the word *depressed*. But he'd had no idea his brother had been keeping a suicide vigil.

"Mom isn't going to kill herself," Sam said. He wasn't sure if he was trying to convince Eddie or himself.

Eddie sat back down on the crate. He looked totally exhausted. There were dark circles under his eyes, and underneath the red blotches his face was pale. "She's like . . . a zombie."

Sam wished he could come up with a good argument to dispute Eddie's description of their mom. He knew he should say something. Something wise and comforting and stable. But nothing came to mind.

"Anyway, I decided I should check in with Dad," Sam said, changing the subject. "But I didn't know how bad it would be . . . so I decided not to take you."

Eddie hung his head. "I'm not a kid," he mumbled.

"I know. . . . I just wanted to see Dad by myself." Sam reached out and gave his brother an awkward pat on the back.

"How is he?" Eddie asked quietly. The anger seemed to have seeped out of him. Hunched over on the crate, he looked more like a ten-year-old than a fifteen-year-old.

"He's doing better than Mom is," Sam answered truthfully. A lot better.

"Is it awful? The jail?" Eddie turned to look at Sam. His eyes were brimming with tears.

Sam cleared his throat. He hadn't cried for years, but the sight of his little brother had put a tennis-ball-size lump in his throat. "It's not so bad," he said.

"Dad was set up," Eddie said fiercely. "He was framed."

Sam didn't answer. He didn't have the heart to tell Eddie the truth. Their father was a criminal. Even worse, he was a criminal without remorse.

"Thanks for coming along for the ride," Dylan said to Natalie. They were in his car, heading up Route 101. Dylan needed to make a run to the printers he had hired to make new menus for the café.

"Are you kidding? I'm having the time of my life." Natalie turned to him and grinned. She *did* look as if she was having fun. Her long dark hair was whipping in the wind, and fresh air had made Natalie's rosy cheeks a shade pinker than usual. "What else do I need besides you, the sun, and a ride in a yellow convertible?"

His thoughts exactly. Dylan saw himself reflected in the mirrored lenses of Natalie's sunglasses. He looked remarkably relaxed, considering the fact that he had just buried himself in debt in order to buy this car. "I think I've figured out a way to write off the whole price of the car as a business expense on my income tax forms," he said.

Natalie laughed. "Leave it to Dylan O'Connor to worry about taxes nine months before they're due to the IRS."

"If I don't worry, who will?" Dylan pointed out.

"Touché," Natalie agreed. "Now tell me about this brilliant plan."

Dylan eased the Olds into the right lane. Their exit was only half a mile away. "I'm going to have Blue and Jason turn the car into a mobile billboard," he explained. "They can paint @café's name across both sides and decorate the hood and the trunk with coffee cups and stuff."

"I love it!" Natalie exclaimed. "@Café will be known all across San Francisco. And you, as the driver of this moving piece of artwork, will become a cult icon. . . . We'll all be famous!"

Dylan laughed. "I'm glad you approve."

Natalie reached over and squeezed Dylan's right hand, which was resting on the large expanse of black leather interior that stretched between them. "I'm proud of you."

He turned his hand palm up and returned the pressure. "Why? What did I do?"

"You're letting life take you to new places," she

70

said. "Example A: You closed the café for my birthday. Example B: You actually danced at Matthew Chance's party. Example C: You bought a car that wasn't *quite* as practical as the minivan you had in mind." She finished the short monologue and gave his hand another light squeeze.

Natalie made his small gestures sound worthy of the Nobel Peace Prize. Dylan usually felt uncomfortable when conversation was centered around himself, but at the moment he felt as if he could listen to Natalie talk about him for hours. "I *am* trying to make some changes," Dylan said. "I want to do more than exist on the planet. . . . I want to feel alive."

"Well, if there's anything I can do to help you in your endeavor, just say the word." Natalie grabbed the top of the windshield and hoisted herself halfway out of her seat. "World, here comes Dylan O'Connor," she yelled into the wind.

There is something you can do, Dylan silently told her. You can kiss me and love me. . . . This was the moment he had been waiting for. They were alone, Natalie was happy, and he was driving a brand-new (to him, anyway) convertible. What better time to tell Natalie his true feelings for her?

Dylan cleared his throat. "Actually—"

Natalie plopped back into her seat. "Do you feel as guilty as I do?" she asked abruptly.

Guilty? Did Natalie felt guilty because she had feelings for him and she thought said feelings were disloyal to Tanya? Or maybe she felt guilty because of the Great Pact. . . . "Uh, guilty about what?" Dylan asked breathlessly.

"Sam." Natalie sighed.

Involuntary frown. This was *not* the response Dylan had been hoping for. "Nat, it's not your fault that Eddie found out about Sam visiting their dad. Sam should have told Eddie about it last week."

"I know . . . but still." She was quiet for a few seconds. "Sam has just seemed so *alone* lately. We should all try to spend more of our free time with him."

Dylan nodded. He agreed—to a point. After Sam's musings about Natalie, Dylan wasn't sure he wanted to encourage Natalie to take the wounded Sam under her nurturing wing. But he would be a terrible person—and an even worse best friend—if he acted on his own agenda.

"That's a great idea," Dylan said. "I'll invite him to hang out tonight." The café closed early on Sunday nights, anyway.

"You're the best friend a guy could have," Natalie said.

Dylan flicked the car's right blinker. Their exit was rapidly approaching. "Thanks, Nat." *I just wish you thought I was the best* boyfriend *a* girl *could have.*

"I think I see him!" Natalie said to Tanya on Sunday night.

"Where?" Tanya hissed. Even though they were

in her mom's Ford Taurus with the windows rolled up, she had insisted on whispering for the last hour and a half.

"Across the street. The guy with the dark glasses."

Tanya snorted. "Hellooo. That guy looks like Urkle from *Family Matters*. Major is Denzel Washington all the way."

"Sorry. I've only met the guy twice. But I'll make sure my Denzel radar is tuned up."

Natalie settled deeper into the passenger seat of the Taurus. Two hours ago Tanya had been struck with the brilliant idea of staking out Major's apartment building. Unfortunately Tanya didn't know where Major lived. She had spent almost an hour calling every Johnson in the phone book until she reached a woman who at least claimed to be Major's mom. Major's mom had given Tanya the address of the apartment in the Castro district, where Major apparently lived with two friends from high school. Now they were parked across the street like two bad detectives in a TV movie.

"I wonder if he's even in there," Tanya said. Her eyes were glued to 111 Diamond Street.

"Maybe he went away for a few days," Natalie said hopefully. This PI stuff was getting old quick.

Tanya flicked her eyes in Natalie's direction. "No. He's in there. I can feel it."

"I have to pee," Natalie said. Maybe a quick run to the nearest gas station would snap Tanya out of this temporary insanity.

Tanya picked up the Big Gulp of diet Coke that

had been resting between her knees. "You can go behind the car," she said, still staring at the apartment building.

Natalie laughed. "Gee, thanks."

Tanya slurped loudly. "Hey, I fed your obsession with Matthew. Now you have to feed mine."

Natalie had never seen Tanya act so . . . uncool about a guy. She was like Mia in that way. Tanya took what she wanted from the stud of the month, then got out without any signs of scarring. Even when Dylan had broken up with her, Tanya hadn't sat around pining about what jerks guys were. She had locked herself in her room with two months' worth of back issues of *People* magazine and several bags of chips, then emerged twenty-four hours later, totally over the whole ordeal.

"You've really got it bad for this guy," Natalie commented. "He must be something special."

Tanya set her empty Big Gulp cup onto the dashboard. "You know how you meet people . . . and it's like they're objects on a shelf?" she asked.

Natalie nodded, although she had no idea where Tanya was going with this particular simile.

"I mean, you look at a guy like he's this knickknack. You make this *list* of his good points and his bad points—as if a person can be boiled down to good hair versus bad manners." She ran her fingers through her long dark curls and glanced at Natalie to make sure she was paying attention. "And based on your careful analysis of the object's advantages and disadvantages, you decide whether to buy it, lease it, or just borrow it for a couple of days."

"Uh-huh . . ." Natalie had never seen Tanya in such a philosophical mood.

"Well, Major *isn't* an object on a shelf. He's like this whole, three-dimensional person all at once. He may have good points. And he may have bad points. But that's all irrelevant. Because he just *is*. . . ."

Natalie whistled. "You've got it bad, T." She recognized the tone of Tanya's voice. It was the same tone Natalie had used in her own mind when she used to think about Dylan. Even though her pining for Dylan had ended ages ago, Natalie could still remember the way she used to marvel at how complete Dylan was. Not like Matthew.

"I think I know what you mean," Natalie said quietly. "I guess I've been looking at Matthew like one of those knickknacks. I want to buy him because he's gorgeous and popular . . . but aside from his shiny surface, I don't really know what he's made of."

Tanya nodded. "You need to find someone else, Nat. A guy who frustrates you . . . and thrills you . . . and makes you feel more like *yourself* than you've ever felt before."

"Does Major do all those things for you?" Natalie asked.

Tanya nodded. "He does—but don't tell anyone."

Natalie grinned. "Your secret is safe with me, sistah."

Tanya nudged Natalie on the arm with her elbow. "So? Are you going to let Matthew go?"

Natalie sighed. "I guess so."

"Good." She grinned. "I'm not sure, but I think we might both be maturing."

Natalie laughed. "Yeah, we're really mature. But somehow I don't think that sitting outside a guy's apartment in your mom's car, scarfing Baked Lay's and drinking diet Coke, is the path toward enlightenment."

Tanya wasn't listening. "Ohmigod!" she squealed. "There he is! It's Major!"

Natalie followed Tanya's gaze. "Boy, I guess I didn't really take a good look at him at Matthew's party. Definitely Denzel-like."

Tanya leaned forward to get a better look. Unfortunately she leaned against the car horn in the process. The horn beeped for two very long seconds. "Damn!" Tanya screeched.

Major turned around. And stared directly at Natalie and Tanya. Natalie slid down low in her seat. This night was about to take an interesting turn. . . .

"Is this great or what?" Dylan said to Sam.

"Awesome," Sam agreed.

Dylan had convinced Sam to go with him to a reading at the giant downtown Barnes &

Noble. They had listened to three young women writers read short stories about rites of passage, and now they were milling around and looking at girls.

"Thanks for making me get out of the house," Sam said. "I know literary readings aren't exactly your scene."

Dylan shrugged. "No problem, bud." As of the end of his conversation with Sam about Natalie, any locale that was going to bring Sam in contact with pretty single girls was Dylan's "scene." And Dylan did have a more pure motivation. He wanted Sam to know that he was there for him.

"This is a serious chick scene." Sam gazed around the room.

Dylan grinned. He had spent half the day trying to figure out the perfect Sam outing. Apparently he had hit the jackpot. There were girls everywhere. The kind of hip, beautiful girls that Sam loved.

"Check out the two lovelies at three o'clock. I think they're giving us The Eye." Sam nodded toward the self-help section of the bookstore.

Dylan glanced at the girls. They were pretty. Very pretty. One brunette, one blonde. Age: roughly eighteen. "Very nice," Dylan said. He wasn't one to extol the virtues of a woman's . . . anatomy.

"Should we work it?" Sam was standing up straighter now. He had the look of a guy who was about to pull out his best line on some unsuspecting female.

"Go for it." Dylan didn't have an interest in talking to either of the girls. But he was glad to see that Sam was still able to enjoy the sight of pretty girls. He wasn't so far gone on Natalie that he had lost his X-ray vision.

"Watch and learn," Sam said. He walked toward the girls.

Dylan followed. He felt like an absolute fool, but Sam seemed happy. That was the important thing. *That* and the fact that Sam hadn't mentioned Natalie once all night.

"Hey, there," Sam said to the blond girl. She was standing next to a shelf of books that seemed to be dedicated to career development.

"Hi," the girl answered. "I'm Sabrina." She pointed at her friend. "This is Nancy."

Dylan flashed his half smile—polite but noncommittal. "Hi."

"We really enjoyed the reading," Sam said in his most intellectual voice. "It's always refreshing to hear from young women writers."

Sabrina's eyes were sparkling. "I'm so glad you said that. . . . Most guys don't appreciate authors like Vivien Tarrow."

Dylan nodded pleasantly. He hadn't particularly enjoyed Vivien Tarrow's diatribe against teenage guys, but he wasn't about to rock the boat. He was too interested in gauging Sam's interest in girls other than Natalie.

"We were just about to go out for some coffee," Sam said. "Why don't you two join us?"

Sabrina looked at Nancy. Nancy looked at Dylan. Dylan looked at the ground. "We'd love to," Sabrina answered.

Dylan smiled. The old Sam was back. Which was good for Sam *and* for Dylan. Sometimes life was all right. Not often . . . but sometimes.

BACK   FORWARD   HOME   STOP

LINK:

Jason Kirk Presents
Saturday Night Live . . .
at the Movies

We all love *Saturday Night Live*—even if it isn't nearly as good as it used to be. I mean, how many times can Alec Baldwin and Steve Martin be on as guest hosts? In recent years the whole cast and crew of *SNL* seems compelled to put out not-so-funny movies based on hilarious TV sketches. Here's a small sampling of what's out there. . . .

The Coneheads: In this romp through the lives of a family cursed (or blessed, depending on your point of view) with funny-shaped heads, Dan Aykroyd and Jane Curtin revamp their famous roles as Mr. and Mrs. Conehead. I'll give this one a marginal thumbs-down, unless you're feeling particularly desperate for cheap laughs.

Wayne's World: Thumbs *way* up on this one, Roger. Mike Meyers and Dana Carvey, as Wayne and Garth, are two of the funniest guys ever to grace the silver screen. And I love their hair! A less enthusiastic thumbs-up goes to *Wayne's World 2*.

Happy Gilmore: In this yuck fest veteran *SNL*er Adam Sandler plays a misguided but lovable golfer. If you're into humor that appeals to the under-age-ten crowd, you'll like this one. Marginal thumbs-up.

It's Pat: One word—bomb. Julia Sweeney, as the gender-neutral Pat, tries hard to make us laugh. But this *isn't* a concept meant to hold our attention for more than a three-minute segment on *Saturday Night Live*. Good try, Julia, but I've got to go thumbs way down on this one. Hey, better luck next time.

Jason will be back next week with a look at movies featuring car crashes.

Monday morning Tanya plunked a decaf cappuccino in front of the much too perky girl at table four. There was nothing more irritating than a person who didn't require caffeine in the morning.

"Would you like your check now or later?" Tanya asked sweetly.

Perky Girl flashed a toothy grin. "Now, please. I have a *million* things I want to get done today."

Tanya ripped the check off her pad and dropped it on the table. "Don't we all."

She turned and headed back to the counter to pick up a tray of five lattes. With the luck she was having lately, Tanya wouldn't be surprised if the whole tray tumbled onto the lap of an unsuspecting customer.

First, Major hadn't called to tell her what a great time he'd had on their date. Second, Natalie had shown up at her house and proceeded to take up residence on the floor of Tanya's room. Natalie's Snoopy sleeping bag, left over from fourth grade, was becoming a permanent piece of furniture. Third, Major still hadn't called. Fourth,

Tanya had had to sit through two days of Natalie telling her what a great friend she was—and what a horrible, rotten sister Mia was. The guilt was like a quickly growing cancer. Fifth, Major still hadn't called. Sixth, the stakeout had been a total bust. Just as Tanya had caught sight of Major, a very large garbage truck had stopped in front of her car and obstructed her view of his very sightly butt. By the time the truck had moved, Major was gone.

At the counter Tanya reached for the tray, but her arms were stopped in midair by a pair of very sexy, dark-skinned hands.

"Stop or I'll shoot," Major whispered in her ear.

Tanya *did* stop, but her heart pounded furiously in her chest. Major was here. Finally. "Oh . . . hey, there." She tried to camouflage the trembling in her voice by clearing her throat.

Major put his hands on Tanya's waist and turned her around so that she was facing him. "Hi." He leaned forward and kissed her softly on the cheek.

It was just a kiss on the cheek. But where Major and lips were concerned, the slightest touch sent Tanya's stomach south for the winter. Several people in the café were staring at them, but Tanya didn't care. She wanted to press her face against Major's chest and not move a muscle for the rest of her shift.

"Is there somewhere we can go?" Major asked.

Tanya nodded as she caught Natalie's eyes. "I'm taking a break," she called.

Natalie flashed her a thumbs-up. "Take twenty."

Tanya clasped Major's hand and led him toward the back room that Dylan had cleared out to make room for his still theoretical kitchen. Maybe her luck was changing. Major had finally showed his face, and for once Dylan wasn't hovering around the café. Tanya didn't need to take a poll to know that Dylan would disapprove of employees (especially her) making out on the premises.

Tanya slipped into the storeroom and perched on the ancient rocking horse that for some reason Dylan hadn't relegated to the city dump. "So."

Major shut the room's door and leaned against it, his arms crossed in front of his chest. "So."

He was staring at her. No, he was staring *into* her. Tanya's heart started to hammer again. She really needed to learn how to keep it together in front of this guy. Of course, as long as he insisted on wearing those perfect-fitting Levi's, she didn't stand a chance. "Are you going to say something?" she finally asked. "Or are you just going to stand there and *look* at me?"

Major grinned. "I haven't decided yet."

If he doesn't kiss me in the next five seconds, I will die. Five, four, three . . . Major walked slowly toward her. "I had fun the other night."

Tanya gulped. Had one of her lungs just collapsed?

83

She couldn't breathe. "Me too," she squeaked. "I mean, it was okay."

Major reached her. He took one of her hands in both of his and rubbed his thumb slowly back and forth across the soft skin of her palm. "Do you want to go out again?"

Speaking was out of the question. Tanya nodded.

Major dropped her hand. "I'll call you."

He headed back across the room. At the door Major turned and gave Tanya another long stare. "By the way, I saw you last night."

Uh-oh. "Uh, where?" Tanya was suddenly very interested in how her manicure was holding up.

"You know where," Major answered. He put his hand on the doorknob. "Sitting across the street from my apartment in your mom's car is cute once—but don't make a habit of it."

Major blew her a kiss and was out the door. Tanya tuned into the loud squeaking of the rocking horse as she swayed back and forth. Any sound was preferable to the alarm bells that were going off in her head.

Major had caught her. And if there had been any question of who had the upper hand before, that question was now answered beyond any and all reasonable doubt. Major had power—and he knew it.

"Want half of my tuna sandwich?" Tanya asked Sam. They were sitting on a bench a few blocks from @café.

"I already ate," Sam answered. Actually he hadn't eaten. But he wasn't hungry. Ever since he had visited his dad in jail, the closest he had come to having an appetite was forcing down a bowl of soup in the middle of the night.

Tanya lifted up her cat-eye sunglasses to look at him. "If you already ate, how come you offered to keep me company during lunch?"

Sam shrugged. "I couldn't stand Eddie anymore. Older brothers and younger brothers were not meant to share the same space for such long periods of time."

Tanya gave him a light punch on the shoulder. "Come on. Eddie's a cute kid. It's good that Dylan gave him a busboy job."

Since Eddie had been hanging around the café with Sam so much, Dylan had finally put him to work. Sam had never seen a kid so excited to clear dirty dishes off sticky tables.

"Don't let Eddie hear you calling him cute," Sam cautioned. "He's probably having erotic dreams about you as it is."

"Sam!" Tanya gave him another punch, then took a bite out of her sandwich.

"Hey, I'm just telling it like it is. I know how the minds of fifteen-year-old boys work . . . I was one."

He was also a seventeen-year-old boy . . . who was still having very unsettling dreams about a beautiful, dark-haired girl who he tried (in vain) to keep nameless in his own head.

Tanya slipped off the sunglasses again. "Does that mean you were having erotic dreams about me when you were fifteen?"

Sam grabbed her diet Coke and took a swig. Man, that stuff was vile. "I thought we were talking about how annoyed I was by the presence of my little brother at the café," he commented.

"We were, we were." She put the sandwich in her lap and threw back her head in a totally Tanya gesture. The girl lived for sunshine.

Sam closed his eyes. Man, he was tired. Brutally, fundamentally tired. For a few minutes he and Tanya sat in silence. It felt good.

"Speaking of erotic, you and Major looked pretty cozy this morning."

Tanya snorted. "Looks can be deceiving. Major and I are a ten-car pileup just waiting to happen."

Sam nodded. Having seen Tanya tear her way through several seemingly solid individuals, he didn't doubt her ability to screw things up. In fact, he could relate to it. There was an overwhelming amount of historical evidence that neither of them was able to sustain a relationship. Which was exactly why Sam knew he was totally insane to be harboring foolish, romantic notions about Natalie.

"I know the feeling," Sam agreed. "Every girl I've dated has ended up thinking I'm the world's biggest jerk."

"I really think I'm ready to settle down," Tanya said. "But Major couldn't be less interested in that particular prospect."

Sam nodded. "I want to change, too. . . . But how can I expect a really awesome girl to give a guy like me a chance?"

Look at last night, Sam said to himself. He had decided over the last few days that Natalie was the only girl who could possibly make him happy. And yet he had asked two strangers to accompany him and Dylan out for a cup of coffee. He had flirted. He had even written down Sabrina's phone number. Then again, as long as he never actually called her, nothing had happened. Just a little casual conversation and a double espresso.

"People change," Tanya observed. "We can't be blamed for our mistakes forever."

"True, true." Maybe Natalie was exactly the person who could change him. If he had Natalie by his side, Sam's dubious reputation would fall away. Once people saw how committed he was to Natalie, no one would doubt that he had the capacity to be a faithful, loyal boyfriend.

Tanya snapped her fingers. "You're my witness, Sam."

"Witness for what?" This should be a good one. Tanya's proclamations were infamous.

"No matter what happens with Major, I'm finished going through guys as if they were paper napkins. From this moment on, I'm a one-guy woman."

Tanya was actually making sense. Build it, and it will come. Right? "Me too . . . that is, from this moment forward I'm a one-woman guy."

Tanya stood up and stuck out her hand. Sam shook it firmly. Tanya obviously believed that Sam was capable of having a relationship. She even seemed to think he deserved to go out with an awesome girl. Who knew? Maybe she was right.

Tanya headed back toward the café. Sam closed his eyes again. For the first time in weeks he felt pretty good. In fact, he felt like a whole new guy. The kind of guy who would make a very good, very stable boyfriend.

There were those moments when nothing short of a major earthquake or an urban avalanche would save one from absolute and total wreckage. Unfortunately the ground wasn't shaking, and nothing seemed to be about to fall on Natalie's head. Why was she cursed with counter duty at this particular juncture in her life? Plan B. Smile and play dumb.

"Hey, Matthew," Natalie said. At least she was pretty sure the words had come out. It was hard to tell, what with all the blood rushing to her head.

"Hi, Nat," Matthew answered. "Nice outfit."

Natalie looked down at herself. Why, oh why had she decided today was the perfect occasion to borrow Tanya's African Queens Are All That T-shirt? "Thanks." What other response was there? "What can I get you?"

"A tall cap." Matthew leaned against the counter, looking every bit as gorgeous as he always did. His dark blond hair was perfectly shaggy, and his jeans (as always) were practically a work of art. Natalie did notice, however, that his chin was just slightly weaker than she had previously thought.

Natalie turned to the cappuccino maker. She really, really hoped that the thing wasn't going to shoot hot foam onto the front of her shirt.

"So, what's up with your sister, anyway?" Matthew asked.

Natalie froze. "Uh, what do you mean?" She couldn't bring herself to turn around to face him.

"She's, like, totally weird."

No kidding. "Yep, that's Mia. Weird." Natalie finished making the cappuccino. She finally turned around and set the paper cup down on the counter. If Matthew thought she was going to stand here and analyze Mia for him, he was even dumber than Dylan kept insisting he was.

Natalie felt a warm, strong hand settle on her waist. "Hey, Nat," Dylan said.

Dylan to the rescue. Again. There wasn't really a good reason to pretend that Dylan was her boyfriend. Matthew obviously couldn't care less *who* Natalie was dating. But then again, it couldn't hurt. "Hi, babe," Natalie said softly.

Natalie glanced over her shoulder to gauge the expression on Matthew's face. Thank goodness, he had the good grace to look confused (it was better than nothing). "Are you guys . . . ?" he asked.

Dylan wrapped his arm around Natalie's shoulders. "Yeah—so don't get any ideas."

Natalie raised her eyebrows. Impressive. Dylan sounded so . . . serious. She'd never realized he was such a good actor.

Matthew handed Natalie a five-dollar bill. "Does Mia have a boyfriend or something?"

Natalie opened the register and pulled out Matthew's change. "Um, I did hear her mention something about David Schwimmer." Hey—anything was possible.

"Or was it Ethan Hawke?" Dylan asked.

Matthew picked up the cappuccino. "Well, when you see her, tell her to give me a call, okay?"

"Sure thing." Natalie didn't think it was necessary to add that she wouldn't have the opportunity to relay his message since she planned never to speak to her sister again.

As Matthew walked out of the café Natalie turned to Dylan. "Shouldn't you be riding a white horse and brandishing a sword?"

Dylan bowed deeply. "My apron is my shining armor."

Natalie laughed, which was an amazing feat, considering the fact that Matthew was *so* unaware of her as potential girlfriend material that he didn't even think it was weird to grill her about her sister. Thank goodness for friends—for Dylan.

Attention: Here's What Natalie Thinks About Families

So we all agree that everyone either has, or had at one time, both a mom and a dad (unless you want to get into the whole cloning thing, which is a totally different story). And some of us are blessed (or cursed, depending on your point of view) with brothers and/or sisters. But what does it all mean?

Everyone says the most important things in life are friends and family. But there's a big difference between the two. We *choose* our friends. Our families are distributed arbitrarily. We're plopped into the world, kicking and screaming, staring up at the faces of those who we'll alternately love and hate for the rest of our lives.

These family relationships are all-consuming and never ending. We study our parents and siblings (especially), wondering, "How can I be so different from these people?"

But since we *are* stuck with the people we get, it's important to try to accept those differences. Your dad likes to sleep standing up? Hey, that's cool. Your mom only eats fried green tomatoes? Oh, well. Your sister is the biggest witch in the world? Try to love her, anyway.

If you're lucky, said family members will grant you the same immunity that you try to grant them. Otherwise you'll all live tied up in knots of frustration until you're old and gray and can't remember what got you so upset in the first place.

Having said this, I'm the first to admit that I don't always manage to "embrace the differences." But I'm working on it. And for now that's good enough for me.

Jason would have laughed if the moment weren't so totally pathetic. He had finally been granted a bona fide full day off work, and where was he? Sitting in a coffee shop. Sure, it wasn't @café. But sipping a latte *anywhere* in this city was hardly a creative way to spend a free afternoon.

Jason had woken up this morning planning a day trip to Mount Tamalpais. And when he had looked out the window at ten A.M., the weather had been perfect—clear skies and warm sunshine. But he had made the mistake of going back to sleep until two o'clock. The weather had changed drastically. Gray skies, chilly wind, and driving rain. Summer in San Francisco was unpredictable at best, downright dismal at worst. So here he was, sitting in a small booth at Java Gaya, coffee cup in hand.

Jason scanned the coffeehouse, comparing it to @café. Dylan's place was bright and comfortable, finished off with a touch of zany. Java Gaya was dark and sensuous. The tables were dark, and the chairs and sofa were upholstered

with varying shades of brocade cloth. In the corner a skinny guy with a guitar was singing folk songs.

Jason opened the small spiral notebook he had stuck in his back pocket. Dr. Grady kept insisting that he should start a journal, but so far Jason hadn't felt moved to record "his thoughts and feelings." He was in the habit of ignoring his inner life—not working to preserve it.

He uncapped the black felt tip pen he had pilfered from his dad's desk. Only one word came to mind. *Blue,* he wrote in large block letters.

"Is that the color or the state of mind?" a husky yet feminine voice asked.

Jason looked up to investigate the source of the question. There was a girl standing next to him. She had long (dyed) red hair, a nose ring, and an incredibly beautiful tattoo of a dragonfly on her left forearm. She was holding a canvas bag, which looked like it might contain anything from tarot cards to baby aspirin. Jason felt as if he had just walked onto the set of a Smashing Pumpkins video.

Tattoo Girl smiled and slid into the booth. "I'm Celia." She held out her hand (which was heavy with silver and turquoise rings) for Jason to shake.

"I'm Jason," he said automatically. "Do I know you?"

"My last name is Dalton." She smiled. "There. Now you know me."

"Okay . . ." Jason shut the spiral notebook. Clearly he was expected to engage in some kind of conversation with this girl . . . Celia.

Celia reached for his coffee cup. She tore open a pack of Equal and dumped it into the coffee. Jason watched in fascination as she took control of the beverage as if it had been hers in the first place.

"You never answered my question," she said. "Is blue a color or a state of mind?" Celia took a sip of coffee and looked at him expectantly.

"Neither," Jason said. "Blue is a person." He couldn't believe he was actually sitting there talking to a stranger about Blue. Okay, he wasn't exactly talking *about* her . . . but still.

Celia opened another packet of Equal. She signaled to the waitress. "Do you want a cup?"

This girl was seriously deranged. "I thought I already *had* one."

She poured the white powder from the Equal packet directly into her mouth. "Easy come, easy go, right?"

Not a bad philosophy, all in all. "I'd like a latte," Jason said to the waitress. "No sugar," he muttered, glancing at Celia.

"So tell me about Blue," Celia said. She flipped her hair over one shoulder, revealing several earrings lined up on her left earlobe.

Jason shrugged. "What do you want to

know?" He must have been in a stranger mood than he had realized. The Jason he lived with every day would have already gotten up, walked away from the table, and headed straight for the door. But he didn't feel like walking out. He felt like forging ahead with this totally bizarre conversation to see what would happen . . . he felt like getting out of his own head and finding out what was in someone else's.

"Male or female?" Celia asked.

"Female." The waitress reappeared and set a fresh latte in front of Jason.

"Girlfriend?"

"Friend." Jason picked up the latte. This was like déjà vu from Saturday night. Then again, Celia looked like a liberated woman. She could probably grasp the concept of platonic relationships.

Celia raised her eyebrows. "Oh, one of *those.*"

"What does one of *those* mean?" Jason asked.

"Let me guess—she's your best friend in the whole world."

"Yeah."

"But you both know that neither of you is the least bit interested in ruining the whole thing by falling into some cheesy romantic trap."

"Yeah." Man, this girl was perceptive.

Celia reached across the table and flipped

open the spiral notebook. She pulled a four-color ballpoint pen out of the small canvas bag, which was now resting in her lap. *Alexander,* she wrote in the same big block letters that Jason had used to write Blue's name.

"So?" Jason asked. "Who's Alexander?"

"Alexander is my own personal Blue," she said. "Correction. He *was.*"

Jason stared at the red ink on the nearly blank page. "He used to be your best friend?"

Celia nodded. "We were best buds. Nothing was going to tear us apart—ever."

"What happened?" Jason asked. He was picturing a horrible car accident or an air conditioner falling on Alexander's head.

"The thing that always happens when a guy and a girl try to be *just* friends. . . . We wound up hating each other."

"Oh." This wasn't good news.

Celia finished her own latte and pulled Jason's fresh cup to her side of the table. "See, a guy and a girl can be best friends for a while, but the whole deal inevitably gets ruined."

Welcome to my nightmare. Who *was* this girl? "Why is that?"

She took a sip of the coffee. "*Because* eventually somebody or other asks if you and the friend of the opposite sex are boyfriend and girlfriend."

"Uh-huh." So far she seemed to know the story of his life.

97

"The thing is, once that idea is planted, it's like this huge *thing* that neither of you can ignore, no matter how hard you try."

Jason was beginning to wish that he had never come into this stupid coffee shop. The atmosphere was undoing all of Dr. Grady's hard work.

Celia was quiet for a moment. She leaned forward in her seat, which caused their respective knees to touch under the table. "Has anyone ever told you that you're incredibly sexy?"

Jason's cheeks felt as if they were on fire. "Uh, no."

She pressed his knee with hers. "Well, you are."

"Thanks." He felt as if he were in a dream. A beautiful girl had just told him that he was sexy.

It was a strange feeling. The only girl he ever talked to was Blue. And she thought he was about as sexy as a plate of turkey surprise from the Alta Vista cafeteria.

"Can I give you a piece of advice?" Celia asked.

Jason shrugged. "Sure." Hopefully she wasn't going to suggest he pierce his eyebrow or tongue or something equally painful.

Celia took the notebook and turned to a fresh page. She drew a large heart. "Get yourself a girlfriend."

Natalie pressed her face close against the black leather of Sam's jacket. The air was cool and windy after the rain that afternoon, but his body was warm and firm. Motorcycles had to be the greatest invention of all time. Natalie felt even freer than she had in Dylan's convertible.

Sam turned the Honda onto a small road that Natalie had never been on before. There were no streetlights, and except for the beam of the single headlight Sam and Natalie were surrounded by the black night.

"Where are we going?" Natalie yelled into the wind.

"You'll see," Sam shouted. He slowed the bike almost to a stop. The sound of rushing wind was abruptly gone.

Several feet away there was a patch of dirt. "There's a little beach down here that I want to show you."

"Wow . . . it's so eerie." Natalie hopped off the back of the Honda. Next to the dirt there was a very steep, very rickety-looking staircase.

Sam slid off the motorcycle and put down the kickstand. "I found this place when I was, like, ten years old," he said. He stood at the edge of the staircase and gazed down at the beach below. "Every Saturday my mom would pack me a bologna sandwich, a minibag of Doritos, and a Coke. I'd take off in the morning and explore all day."

"That sounds great," Natalie said softly. Sam's voice was so sad . . . as if he had been ten years old decades ago.

"It was." He started down the long staircase without another word.

Natalie zipped up her blue Patagonia shell jacket and followed. Sam had been acting strange all day. He had brought Eddie to the café this morning, then sat for six hours at a corner table, scribbling on a legal pad. Around three o'clock Sam had taken Eddie home, then come straight back to the café.

At the end of her shift Sam had offered Natalie a ride home. But instead of taking her straight to Tanya's (her current home away from home), he had suggested a ride up the coast. Natalie had been thrilled by the idea. She loved Tanya—but the expression "too much of a good thing" had definitely been running through her mind for the past couple of days. And Natalie suspected that Tanya wasn't totally grooving on the concept of a permanent roomie.

"We're here," Sam said. The last step of the staircase was about three feet above the ground. Sam jumped onto the beach.

Natalie clasped Sam's outstretched hand and leapt after him. "Beautiful!"

The beach was totally deserted. To the north there was a large cluster of trees, and to the south there was an old lighthouse. Scattered over the sand were large rocks and boulders. Natalie closed her eyes. She could imagine lying on one of those boulders at noon, in the hot summer sun, basking in the warmth of the day.

"Look up," Sam said. He was still holding her hand.

Natalie gazed at the sky. In San Francisco the city lights obscured the stars. But tonight she could see the entire galaxy painted on the black night sky. "It's like being on a field trip at the planetarium," she said.

Sam chuckled. "Yeah—but there's no one kicking the back of your seat or snapping their gum at a deafening volume."

Sam sank onto the hard-packed sand. "Sometimes I wish I could just pitch a tent, build a fire, and spend every night out here."

"Why don't you?" Natalie asked. She plopped down beside Sam, close enough so that she could enjoy the warmth emanating from his body. This place was spectacular—but chilly.

High in the sky the wind blew a small cloud westward, revealing a large full moon. "I can't," Sam responded, staring up at the moon. "I've learned the definition of that evil word—responsibility—and I can't figure out a way to unlearn it."

Natalie nodded. "Maybe you could bring Eddie here with you," she suggested. "He'd probably give anything to camp out with his older brother."

Sam shook his head. "Eddie isn't the problem. It's my mom."

"Is she in really bad shape?" Natalie asked softly.

Sam didn't respond right away. "She's . . . lost," he said finally. "The other morning Eddie found her asleep at the kitchen table. When we woke her up, she promised that she was going to get her life back together."

"What happened?" Natalie didn't want to probe Sam for the grim details, but he seemed as if he wanted to talk.

"Nothing—she's been holed up in her bedroom ever since. I don't think she's even taken a shower in a week."

"She's had a rough time, Sam. You all have. Give her some time." Natalie reached out and put her arm around Sam's shoulders. She had never seen him so utterly defeated.

"Where did it all go wrong, Nat?" Sam asked. He shifted on the sand so that their bodies were touching. His head came down to rest on her shoulder.

"I don't know," she said. "Families are mysterious beasts. Look at mine . . . my mom died when I was so young that I barely remember her. And Mia and I are enemies."

Sam sat up straight again. "You can't change the fact that your mother died, Nat. But this war with Mia is senseless. Matthew Chance isn't worth this grief."

Natalie was beginning to think Sam's point of view was right. Her life wasn't over because Matthew didn't want to be her boyfriend. And Matthew himself had said that Mia hadn't returned his phone calls. It was possible—maybe—that Mia respected Natalie's feelings and was staying away from Matthew on purpose.

"She makes me so angry," Natalie said. "It's not even her fault . . . it's just . . ."

"Family," Sam finished.

Natalie nodded. Life was so complicated—and so fundamentally disappointing. "But we're talking about you—not me," she reminded him.

Sam turned his head so that he was looking into Natalie's eyes. "Thanks, Nat."

"For what?" Sam's brown eyes were brimming with tears, and his voice was low and husky.

"For being . . . you." He reached for her hand and squeezed it tightly.

Natalie brushed her fingers against his cheek. "I'm glad being me is something that fills you with gratitude. . . . I'm used to trying to be anything *but* me."

Sam shook his head. "You don't even understand how . . ." His voice trailed off, and he looked out into the ocean.

"How what?" Natalie asked. Sam was always intense, but tonight he had entered a whole new realm. She had never seen him this way. Ever.

Sam glanced down at their intertwined hands, then stared into Natalie's eyes. "How wonderful you are," he whispered.

"Thanks," she whispered back.

Sam shifted his position so that they were sitting face-to-face. "I want to kiss you right now," he said softly. "I want to kiss you very, very badly."

The natural biorhythms of Natalie's body were suddenly thrown entirely out of whack. She hadn't heard what she thought she'd heard. *I want to* assist *you,* he must have said. Or, *If you ever go away to college, I'll* miss *you.* Some bird must have trilled at the exact moment when Sam was saying . . . that word.

"What did you say?" Natalie squeaked.

Sam leaned close. "I want to kiss you."

"Oh . . ." Natalie gave herself a covert pinch on the arm. This whole conversation had to be either a dream or a hallucination.

"May I?" Sam asked. His voice was quiet but insistent.

"Sam, I . . . this is crazy." She resisted the urge to start giggling uncontrollably. "We're friends. . . . I mean, you're just upset about your dad—"

Natalie's next words died in her throat. Sam closed the rest of the space between them. He touched her lips softly with his. Once. Twice. Three times. The sensation was startling . . . totally alien and familiar at the same time. She should pull away. She should laugh. She should . . . what? Sam kissed her again, but this time she allowed her lips to soften . . . and the kiss lingered. His hands closed around her shoulders, then moved into her long tangled hair.

I'm going to let this happen, she realized. She had been alone and untouched for so long . . . forever. She wanted to be wanted. In Sam's words, she wanted that very, very badly.

BACK FORWARD HOME STOP

LINK:

Tanya Talks Makeup Tips

All of you probably haven't had the chance to read *Cindy Crawford's Basic Face,* my pick for best book of the year. Just kidding, but it is a cool read. And talk about makeup tips! Cindy knows everything there is to know about foundation, blush, and lipstick. I've decided to take it upon myself to share some of Cindy's best tips with you. If you like what you see, support Cindy and go buy her ultrahip glamour book. . . .

Accentuate the positive. This particular tip is perhaps more philosophical than practical, but it's definitely right-on. Instead of trying to cover up what you hate (whether it's your eyes or lips or whatever), draw attention to what you *like* (or at least what you can stand to look at in the mirror). If you love your eyes, load on the mascara. Dig your lips? Let's see some bright red lipstick on those babies. You get the idea.

Blend. Cindy uses this word again and again. Blend *everything.* A line of foundation cutting across the bottom of your cheek does *not* look good. That goes for blush and eyeliner, too. The idea is to look at least seminatural. Not to look like a clown from the Big Apple Circus.

Don't smoke. You already know all the bad stuff about smoking—how it ruins your lungs and gives you cancer and emphysema and all that good stuff. Smoking also causes wrinkles, which no amount of makeup can really hide.

Apply makeup in natural light. This is fairly self-explanatory. What looks good under the glaring light above your bathroom mirror may not be so flattering once you get outside into the real world.

That's all. Happy makeovers, everybody!

Blue pressed tentatively on the brake pedal of her mother's maroon Toyota hatchback. She had finally obtained her driver's license (after failing the test twice) three months ago. But she hadn't put in much actual driving time since. Blue couldn't imagine being comfortable behind the wheel of two tons of steel. She stopped at the red light at the bottom of Jones Street. Okay, time to regroup for the final stretch to the Kirks' house.

Of course, she might be a better driver if her lessons hadn't been so haphazard. Dylan had insisted that he was a better driving teacher than any certified instructor. But Blue had quickly realized that patience (at least in the driving department) was *not* one of her older brother's virtues. He had guided her calmly through a couple of spins around a giant, empty parking lot behind Safeway, then expected her to ease into heavy traffic like a pro.

But around nine P.M. Blue had decided it was time she took the horse by the reins (so to speak) and ventured into night driving. The fact that she was out on the street

NINE

had nothing to do with the fact that she hadn't seen Jason once all day. Or *talked* to him, for that matter.

Okay, maybe that *was* why she had decided now was the perfect time to negotiate the hilly, windy roads of San Francisco. But it was imperative that she and Jason reestablish the rhythm of their easygoing banter.

When Blue had left Jason's the other night, she had felt even more disconcerted than she had the night after Matthew's party. Three weeks ago—even one week ago—Blue wouldn't have believed that something as utterly stupid as an ill-fated blind date and a few people thinking they were a boyfriend-girlfriend combo would throw her into a totally discombobulated fit. She couldn't live like this.

The light turned green. Blue inched the Toyota into the intersection and turned left onto Franklin Street. It wasn't weird that she was arriving at Jason's unannounced at nine-thirty at night. Jason popped up under *her* window all the time.

Blue picked up speed as she headed up Franklin. Unfortunately the Kirks' house appeared more quickly than she had expected. Blue slammed on the brakes and came to a screeching halt directly in front of their front path. Mission accomplished (more or less).

Blue slid out of the car and banged the driver's side door shut. She jogged up the path and pressed her finger against the doorbell. The first bars of Beethoven's Fifth rang out. Blue smiled, remembering how mortified Jason had been when Rachel insisted the Kirks install a novelty doorbell.

The door swung open. "Hey, Blue." Rachel was standing in the foyer, holding a bottle of black nail polish.

"Hi, Rachel. Is Jason around?"

"Upstairs." She stepped back to let Blue inside. "Can you shut the door? I don't want to mess up my nails." She held out her freshly painted fingernails for Blue to inspect. "Cool, huh?"

"Yeah . . . cool." Blue wasn't a big fan of nail polish. How did girls have the patience to sit around—totally incapacitated—while they waited for the polish to dry?

Blue walked through the house, heading for the back staircase, which led straight to Jason's second-floor bedroom. She wasn't going to make a big deal about the fact that he didn't even mention Dylan had given him a day off. And she wasn't even going to bring up the fact that he didn't stop by the café to visit her. Blue knocked softly on Jason's door.

"Enter at your own risk," Jason called.

Blue pushed open the door. "It's me."

Jason was sitting in an ancient La-Z-Boy chair that he had inherited when his mother had revamped the family room several years ago. The chair was the centerpiece of Jason's eclectic room.

He had painted two walls black and two white, all four of which were covered with movie posters he had accumulated over the past couple of years. His bed was a small twin, which he kept shoved in the furthest corner of the room.

"Hey, there," Jason said. "I was just thinking about calling you."

A disturbing shiver of pleasure traveled up Blue's spine. Since when did the fact that Jason was thinking about dialing her number make her day? She shrugged. "I guess I'm psychic."

Jason heaved himself out of the La-Z-Boy. "Have a seat."

"Thanks." Blue plopped into the chair and put her feet up on the attached footrest. "So, where've you been all day?"

Jason flopped onto his bed. "I was . . . around. I hung out at Java Gaya for a while."

"Why didn't you come by the café?" She couldn't help herself. She had to ask the question.

Jason threw a couple of pillows up against the wall and leaned back. "I'm kinda burnt on the place, you know?"

What about me? Are you burnt on me, too?
"Yeah . . . I know what you mean."

"How did you get—"

"How was the—" Blue said at exactly the same time. They both laughed. "Coffee shop?" she finished.

"Java Gaya is pretty cool, I guess. . . . I met a really bizarre girl there."

"Really?" Blue asked. Jason had never met a girl in his life. Well, sure, he had *met* them. But he had never made a point of telling her about it.

He nodded. "Her name is Celia, and she's, like, totally overwhelming."

"Uh, overwhelming good—or overwhelming bad?" Blue tilted the La-Z-Boy back as far as it would go.

He shrugged. "Just . . . overwhelming." He put his hands behind his head and stared up at the ceiling. "I mean, she just, like, sat down and started talking to me like we were best friends or something."

Blue hated Celia. She knew that instinctively. "This girl sounds like a wack job."

"She is. She said, like, the craziest stuff." He sounded amused, sort of as if he was re-membering some private joke that he and nut-girl had shared. "We talked for, like, three hours."

"Like what? What did she say?" Was that whiny, nagging voice hers? Impossible.

Jason shook his head. "It's so dumb. . . . I mean, jeez."

Now Blue really was getting irritated. Since when was Jason so coy? "Come on, spit it out," she ordered.

"Well, she said she thought I should, like, find a girlfriend . . . or something." His face was turning slightly pink.

111

Blue snorted. "I hope you told her off. . . . That's the stupidest thing I've ever heard."

"Yeah." His tone was noncommittal.

"So?" Blue urged. "Did you tell her she had no idea what she was talking about? Did you explain that you don't go in for all that cheesy, revolting boyfriend and girlfriend stuff?"

"Sure, I mean, yeah." He sat up straight on the bed. "This is a dumb conversation."

"I'll second *that* emotion," Blue snapped. She couldn't believe she had braved the urban jungle just to talk about some freaky chick with an attitude problem.

"So," Jason said.

"So." There was a long pause. And then the pause went on. And on.

Blue stood up to leave. Apparently Jason had an easier time communicating with complete strangers than he did with her. She felt as if she were sinking into a long multipart nightmare.

"Tanya?" Natalie called softly. "Are you awake?" She was nestled in the Snoopy sleeping bag that had been serving as her bed for the past few nights.

The only sound coming from Tanya's bed was even, steady breathing. I'm not going to wake her up. I am *not* going to wake her up. "Tanya!" Natalie's voice was louder this time.

"Huh?" Tanya's response was more of a grunt than an utterance, but Natalie was prepared to take anything she could get.

The Kiss was playing over and over in her mind, and there was no way she was going to be able to close her eyes, much less fall asleep, until she got Tanya's input on the whole situation.

"Are you awake?" Natalie asked.

Tanya turned over. "I am now." She didn't sound happy about the fact. As an only child, Tanya wasn't accustomed to having her daily routine interrupted by an outside party.

"I have to talk to you," Natalie said. "I'm, like, losing my mind."

"You've got five minutes." Tanya propped herself up with a couple of pillows. "Then I'm going back to sleep. I was having the most amazing dream about Major. We were in his car—"

"This is serious, T.," Natalie interrupted. "Something pretty big happened tonight." She wriggled herself up into a sitting position.

"What?" Tanya sounded wide awake now.

"Sam kissed me." Natalie hadn't realized just how shocking that fact was until she heard herself saying the words aloud.

"Excuse me—I didn't hear you right." Tanya slapped the side of her head as if she were trying to shake water out of her ear.

"Yeah, you did," Natalie informed her. "Sam kissed me."

"No *way!*" Tanya squealed. "You're lying!"

Natalie shook her head. "Girl Scout's honor."

Tanya clutched her heart. "You're serious."

"Yep." The fact that Tanya was having such a hard time believing that a guy had kissed Natalie wasn't exactly flattering. But she knew Tanya's reaction was based on the *who* not the *what*.

"Wow . . . ," Tanya breathed. "Our Sam? Sam Bardin?" Her voice was sort of high and squeaky.

"You got it." Natalie grinned in the darkness. She was actually enjoying this role reversal. Usually it was Tanya telling Natalie about all the exciting events in *her* life. It was nice to have her own juicy story to deliver. "But you have to promise not to tell anyone."

Tanya switched on the light beside her bed. "When? Where? Why?"

Man, where should she start? The motorcycle ride? The beach? The Kiss itself? "It was like, I mean, we were at this beach . . . and then, like, we were talking—"

"Nat, you're making about as much sense as Robin Williams on a sugar rush. Just start at the beginning—calmly."

"Okay, here goes. . . ." Natalie took a deep breath. "After work Sam and I went on a motorcycle ride and ended up at this little beach he used to go to when he lived in Sausalito."

"So far it sounds a little out of the ordinary, but not mind-blowing," Tanya commented.

"Right. My thoughts exactly."

"Continue," Tanya urged. "This is better than *The Young and the Restless.*"

"Well, we started talking about his family and then *my* family, and then . . ." Her voice trailed off.

"Don't stop now," Tanya said. "I sense that we're getting to the good part."

Natalie pulled the sleeping bag up around her shoulders. "And then . . . he kissed me."

She still felt that kiss—those kisses—on her lips. And she remembered Sam's eyes when he had finally pulled away. Before tonight she had never noticed the gold flecks in his dark brown eyes.

"He just, like, kissed you? Out of nowhere?" She sounded incredulous.

"It wasn't out of nowhere—" Or was it? "I think he's just going through a rough time. And I was there and he was there. . . ."

"Did you kiss him back?" Tanya leaned forward and wiggled her eyebrows.

"Not at first." Natalie's cheeks were growing warm. "But then I did."

Tanya whistled. "Well, well, well. Natalie the Kissing Bandit emerges from the depths."

Natalie groaned. "The whole thing was so surreal. A week ago I was positive that Matthew and I were going to be a couple. Now I've kissed Sam Bardin. . . . It doesn't make any sense."

"Did you guys, like, declare your love for each other or what?" Tanya asked.

"No!" Natalie screeched. "We just . . . kissed."

"And then what?" Tanya leaned forward, almost falling out of the bed in anticipation.

Natalie closed her eyes. She and Sam had stayed on the beach, kissing and kissing. And then a cold wind had blown over them, and Natalie had shivered. The moment was over. And they had stopped kissing. They had climbed up the rickety old staircase in silence. And in silence they had climbed onto Sam's motorcycle. Natalie had held tight to Sam's leather jacket as he had sped down the highway and through the deserted streets of San Francisco.

"We stopped kissing, and then he drove me here." She had slipped off the back of the bike and given him a soft kiss on the cheek. *See you tomorrow,* Sam had said. The words had been casual but ripe with promise. Or had they? And if they *had,* did she want them to be?

"So . . . what happens now?" Tanya leaned back into her pillows.

"I don't know," Natalie whispered. "I just don't know."

"Do you like him?" Tanya asked. "I mean, could you, like, potentially fall in love with the guy?"

"Maybe . . ." Natalie's voice trailed off. This was all so confusing.

"I hear a 'but' at the end of that sentence."

"Well, look at you and Dylan," Natalie said. "You guys were awesome friends, and then you went out . . . and then you broke up . . . and

116

nothing will ever be quite the same between you again."

"True."

"Do you think that's what would happen with Sam and me?" Natalie wanted Tanya's answer to be no. She wanted Tanya to tell her that she and Sam were a perfect couple who were meant to fall in love, get married, and live happily ever after.

"I don't know," Tanya said quietly. "Only you and Sam can know the answer to that question."

"Is romance always this complicated?" Natalie felt as if her brain had been put into a high-speed blender.

Tanya laughed. "Obviously something very important did happen tonight, Nat, but it wasn't the simple act of you kissing Sam."

"What was it?" Natalie couldn't imagine anything more significant than that.

"You've joined the Relationship Club. You've realized that there's no such thing as a sure bet. Things happen when they happen . . . and there's no way to predict the outcome." Tanya turned off the light and lay back down in bed.

"I don't know if I can take all this ambiguity," Natalie said. "Having a crush on Matthew from afar was a lot easier than having something *real* with Sam."

"I'm so happy for you, I could cry," Tanya said dramatically. "This is *huge.* . . . This is serious."

Natalie sat in the dark, staring out of Tanya's window into the moonlit night. She had gotten what she wanted tonight. A sexy, intelligent, cool guy had looked at her—*Natalie*—and wanted to touch her. He had wanted to put his arms around her and run his fingers through her hair and whisper into her ear.

She should be happy. She should feel like staying up all night and writing poems and singing seventies love tunes in her head. And she *was* excited. But she was also curiously empty.

Natalie closed her eyes. She would figure all of this out tomorrow. Tomorrow everything would be clear. Or at least . . . different.

"I'm coming. I'm coming!" Dylan shouted. Some extremely annoying individual was pounding on the door of his studio apartment. Dylan pulled a sweatshirt over his head as he stumbled the rest of the way to the door. He had been in the middle of a very satisfying dream about Natalie when he had been woken up by the sound of knuckles hitting against the hollow wood of his front door.

Dylan flipped back the dead bolt lock and pulled open the door. "What?" he yelled.

"Hey, man." Sam was standing under the fluorescent light in the hallway.

Dylan blinked as his eyes adjusted to the

sudden onslaught of light. "What the hell are you doing here?"

Sam walked into the tiny apartment. "I couldn't sleep."

"Have you ever heard of counting sheep?" Dylan asked.

"I'm not even *near* sleep," Sam answered. "Counting sheep isn't going to do the trick."

"So you decided to wake me up in the middle of the night." Dylan shut the door behind Sam.

It was entirely possible that he was in for a long night of listening to Sam ramble. But that was fine. After all, what were friends for?

Sam was circling the room. "Sorry, man," he said, crossing the length from the kitchen to the bathroom in four long strides. "But I really need to talk."

Dylan headed toward the kitchen to make a pot of coffee. Unless he pumped some caffeine into his blood, Sam's soul baring was going to be greeted by the sound of snores. "I'm glad you felt like you could come to me," Dylan called as he retrieved a chipped yellow mug from one of his two miniature cabinets. "I really want to, uh, be here for you." Dylan was grateful that he didn't have to look Sam in the face as he said all this mushy stuff. "Want some coffee?"

"No, thanks," Sam said. "I'm already way past wired."

Dylan stuck his minicoffeepot under the faucet. "If you want to go ahead and, uh, start talking about stuff . . . I'm listening." He pulled a

119

small bag of hazelnut grounds out of the freezer.

Sam sighed heavily. "I don't know where to start, man. Tonight was just *so* totally insane."

Dylan measured out two tablespoons of coffee and dumped it into a filter. "Did something happen to your mom? Is she okay?" He pushed the start button on the coffeemaker.

"For once my mind is on something besides my dysfunctional family." Sam was still walking around the small room as if he were doing laps around a track.

"Well, sit down and tell me what *is* on your mind. All that pacing is making me nervous."

Sam sank onto the folding metal chair that was the closest thing Dylan had to a piece of comfortable furniture. He rubbed his hands back and forth across his head, causing his dark brown hair to stand straight up. "I don't even know where to start."

Dylan headed back to the kitchen to check on the progress of his coffee. "Start at the beginning."

"I was born in Saint Joseph's hospital in—"

"Ha, ha," Dylan interrupted from the kitchen. "I mean start at the beginning of whatever it is you're dying to tell me."

"I guess I might as well come right out and say it. . . ."

Dylan grabbed the coffeepot and carried it over to his mug. "*Please,* just say it. I'm dying of suspense here."

"I kissed Natalie tonight. . . . Well, we kissed

120

each other, actually." Sam's voice was practically trembling with excitement.

The coffeepot shook in Dylan's hand. Hot liquid poured over his left hand. "Ouch!" Dylan yelled. "Damn!"

Sam had kissed Natalie. Natalie had kissed Sam. Maybe he wasn't awake at all. Maybe this whole episode had been a horrible nightmare. Right. If it weren't for the searing pain in his left hand, he could *almost* believe that was true. Sam had kissed Natalie. Natalie had kissed Sam. Dylan was going to vomit.

Sam appeared at the door of the kitchen. "Are you all right?"

Dylan put the coffeepot in the sink. The skin below his thumb and index finger was bright red. He turned on the cold water and stuck his hand underneath it. "Fine. Fine."

"Did you hear what I said?" Sam asked. "Natalie and I kissed!"

Say something, Dylan ordered himself. Respond to this statement in some semirational manner. "Yeah, I heard you the first time." The water wasn't cold enough to numb the pain in his hand. Or the pain anywhere else in his body, for that matter.

"Is that wild news or what?" Sam opened the door of the fridge.

Smile. Be nice. Punch the slimy grin off his smug face. "That's one word for it, anyway."

"Do have any juice or something?" Sam was leaning into the refrigerator. Dylan suppressed the urge to give him a hard kick in the butt.

121

"There's a bottle of seltzer water," Dylan answered, using all his mental powers to keep the rising tide of hatred he felt for Sam out of his voice.

Sam grabbed the seltzer. He banged the refrigerator door shut. "Now is when you give me a high five and shout, 'Way to go!'"

Dylan turned off the water. "I'm not sure that you taking advantage of Natalie merits a high five." He turned away from Sam and headed into the other room. He definitely didn't need coffee now. Dylan was far more alert than he cared to be.

"I didn't take *advantage* of her. . . . It just happened." Sam had followed Dylan into the main room of the apartment. Instead of reclaiming the metal chair he plopped onto Dylan's futon, which was currently folded out into its "bed" position.

Dylan took the other chair. "Is it going to happen *again?*" Please, God, let the answer be no. Please. Please. Please.

"I sure hope so." Sam was staring vacantly at the ceiling. This really stupid, immature grin had spread across his face.

"Did you guys, like, talk about your . . . feelings?" Dylan asked. His heart was skipping approximately one out of every three beats.

Sam took a long gulp of seltzer. "We talked about everything, Dylan. . . . It was incredible."

"Sounds pretty intense." Dylan could barely choke out the words.

"We were sitting on the beach. It was dark and

122

beautiful and there were a million stars." Sam sighed (with ecstasy, in Dylan's opinion). "Natalie reached for my hand, and then I—"

Natalie had touched *him*. She had pursued a voluntary impulse to make physical contact with Sam. He hadn't happened upon her in the middle of a nap and planted one on her. She had been an active participant in the whole event. Oh, God. It was possible—probable, even—that Natalie was in love with Sam.

"Spare me the details." Dylan didn't think he could bear to hear the blow-by-blow account of what went on. He was barely handling the general overview.

Sam didn't appear to be listening. "Natalie is so understanding. When I talk to her, I feel almost like a human being again . . . and those lips. Wow!"

"What about the Great Pact?" Dylan asked. Finally some negative aspect of this he could cling to for dear life. "We all had an agreement."

Sam scoffed. "The Great Pact can bite me."

Clearly guilt wasn't going to be an effective means to end this thing before it went any further. "Natalie isn't like the other girls you've gone out with," Dylan said, choosing his words carefully. "It wouldn't be fair to lead her on."

Sam leaned forward. "Don't you get what I'm saying? Natalie is the *only* person who makes me feel better about the whole thing with my parents. She's, like, this guardian angel sent to guide me through the abyss that my life has become."

What could Dylan say to that? Sam deserved some joy in his life right about now. Did Dylan really want to sabotage his best friend's only hope for happiness because the two of them happened to be in love with the same woman?

Yes, he did. But I'm not going to, he vowed to himself. "I'm happy for you, Sam." The words were like rocks in the back of his throat. "I hope it all works out the way you want."

"Thanks, man." Sam leaned back in the futon and closed his eyes.

Dylan wished his apartment were on a higher floor. He felt like plunging to his death in a dramatic, romantic leap from his front window.

Focus, Dylan commanded himself. Be enthusiastic. Be supportive. "So are you guys going to go on a . . . date . . . anytime soon?" Dylan asked.

There was no response. Dylan had been staring at the floor, but now he glanced at Sam. Great. Sam's mouth was hanging wide open, and he was breathing deeply. "Sam!" Dylan called.

Nothing. Dylan was stuck with Sam peacefully asleep on his bed while he himself was sure to be up all night trying to figure out what had just happened. Dylan stood up and grabbed one of the blankets off his futon. He might as well get comfortable (as comfortable as one could be) on the metal folding chair.

He had a long, bleak night to look forward to. Scratch that. He had a long, bleak *life* to look forward to.

Sardyhey:	Hello? Is anyone in here?
Tina554:	Of course there are people here. This is the coolest chat room.
Gregyikes:	You're just saying that 'cause you started it.
Dylan987:	Hi, people.
Alliecat12:	Can we have some kind of directed conversation, please?
Sardyhey:	Does anyone know how I can get a fake ID?
Tina554:	Great idea, Allie. Someone start a convo.
Dylan987:	I'm miserable. My best friend kissed the girl I love.
Gregyikes:	Go to any college campus, Sardy. Fakes galore.
Alliecat12:	That's so sad, Dylan. I'm sorry.
Tina554:	Poor Dylan. You sound like a sensitive guy.
Dylan987:	The thing is, my friend is going through a bad time. I should be happy for him. Not jealous and hateful.
Gregyikes:	Tough break, man.
Sardyhey:	Maybe Tina or Allie will fill that aching void for you.
Dylan987:	Should I tell him how I feel? Should I tell her?
Alliecat12:	If it's meant to be between you two, it'll happen.
Tina554:	Try to find someone else. It's the only answer.
Gregyikes:	Enough of this sappy talk. I'm gagging.
Dylan987:	I can't even think about anyone else. I'm in love with her.

Sardyhey:	Tina, do you want to meet each other in person?
Alliecat12:	Maybe you should write her a letter if it's that important.
Tina554:	I already have a boyfriend, Sardy. Sorry!
Shrkeatr7:	You're all totally lame. I'm going to an adult room.
Dylan987:	I guess I'll just wait and see what happens. Or die.
Alliecat12:	I'm single, Sardy.
Gregyikes:	Later, dudes and dudettes. I'm not into this Hallmark stuff.
Sardyhey:	Really, Allie? What do you look like?
Tina554:	Dylan, are the guy and girl in love with each other?
Dylan987:	Maybe I *should* write her a letter. . . .
Tina554:	You really sound like a great guy, Dylan.
Alliecat12:	You're a pig, Sardy. Do you have to ask about my looks?
Dylan987:	Thanks, Tina. I guess "great" isn't enough.
Sardyhey:	Sorry, Al. Didn't mean to be so superficial.
Tina554:	Love is so tough. But it can be awesome, too.
Sardyhey:	As they say, there are lots of fish in the sea, Dylan.
Alliecat12:	You can E-mail me, Sardy, if you really want to.
Dylan987:	Good night, everyone. Thanks for listening.
Tina554:	Night, Dylan. Don't despair.
Sardyhey:	Later, dude. Keep the faith.

"Dad!" Natalie exclaimed Tuesday morning. "What are you doing here?"

Her nerves had been totally and completely frayed since she arrived at the café at nine o'clock. Every time she turned around, Natalie expected to see Sam walk through the door. And she had less than no idea how she was supposed to act when she saw him. Now seeing her dad at eleven o'clock on a Tuesday morning was throwing her *way* out of whack.

Mr. van Lenton glanced uneasily around the interior of @café. He was a great father, but he had never been comfortable around large groups of "young people." "I had a sudden craving for a decaf mocha latte," he said casually. "So here I am."

Natalie rolled her eyes. "Dad, I've been working here over a year. And you have *never* stopped by for a coffee. Not once."

Mr. van Lenton adjusted the conservative, blue-and-red-striped tie around his neck. "You caught me, hon." He paused. "I actually want to talk to you about coming home."

Natalie started to make her dad the decaf mocha latte. As long as he was here he might as well sample the

127

goods. "I've been thinking a lot about that very issue," Natalie said.

"I try to stay out of whatever squabbles you and Mia have, but this time I feel I must speak up." He ran his hands through his thinning, sandy brown hair as he searched for the right words. "All I know is that you and Mia had a disagreement over some boy. . . . Now, I know that emotions are very volatile at your age, but you simply *cannot* stay at Tanya's house until it's time for you to go away to college—"

"You're right, Dad," Natalie interrupted. "I'm coming home tonight."

Late last night Natalie had realized that her cold war with her sister was both stupid and irrelevant. Matthew Chance wasn't important enough to make her uproot herself and sever all family ties. He was just a dumb (but good-looking) jock who had happened across her path at a time when she was seeking a new identity.

And as much as she hated to admit it to herself, there was just the *smallest* chance that she had overreacted to Mia's actions. Natalie had never actually *told* Mia that she was interested in (okay, obsessed with) Matthew. And even though Natalie liked to blame Mia for the fact that guys were constantly drooling all over her, it wasn't Mia's fault that she was blessed with Niki Taylor's genes.

Mr. van Lenton didn't appear to have heard Natalie's statement. "At the moment Mia is away on a photo shoot in Portland," he continued. "Come home tonight, and then you'll still have a day or two

128

to cool off before you two have to sleep under the same roof. . . ."

"You're right," Natalie repeated. "I'll see you around eight o'clock."

"Families are so important," Mr. van Lenton went on. "Someday you'll value your relationship with your sister—"

"Dad!" Natalie shouted. She snapped her fingers in front of his face.

"Yes?" He looked slightly confused.

"I *said* I'm coming home." Natalie couldn't help laughing.

"Great!" Mr. van Lenton's face transformed as he grinned at Natalie. "I'm glad you appreciated what I had to say."

There was no point explaining that she had already made up her mind last night to move back into her own bedroom. Her dad was clearly proud of the moving speech he had just made. Natalie handed him a decaf mocha latte to go. "Me too, Dad."

Mr. van Lenton leaned across the counter and gave her a kiss on the cheek. "I'll see you tonight, Nat."

"Bye, Dad." Natalie watched as her suit-clad father negotiated his way past several tables full of teenagers. He pushed open the door and headed out into the bright sunshine.

Natalie grinned at Dylan, who was busing table two. "I'm moving back into my house," she told him.

Dylan gave her a cold smile. "Good for you," he

said with the same amount of enthusiasm she would expect from a doctor who was informing her she had a brain tumor the size of a golf ball.

Natalie frowned. "Is it just me, or is it chilly in here?"

Dylan didn't respond. He turned from the table and stalked toward the storeroom. The grin fell from Natalie's face. What had started out as the first day of the rest of her life was obviously not going to be the happy-ending episode of *The Brady Bunch* that she had hoped.

Tuesday afternoon Sam stared at himself in the small mirror above the sink of the guys' bathroom in @café. "Do you want to catch a movie tomorrow night?" he asked himself. Too casual.

He cleared his throat. "May I have the pleasure of your company at dinner tomorrow evening?" Too formal.

"Would you like to go on a date with me after work sometime?" Sam tried to strike a friendly-yet-romantic tone of voice. That could be okay. He would state his intention but remain (more or less) coolly detached. If Natalie wanted to turn him down, she could.

"Just do it," Sam ordered himself. Man, he had never noticed what a big forehead he had before. And his eyes were, like, *really* close together.

Someone pounded on the door. "What's going on in there?" Dylan shouted. "A convention?"

Sam cringed. When he had woken up on Dylan's futon this morning, his best friend had been huddled in a sheet and half dozing in his small bathtub—Dylan had said that considering the number of cockroaches that liked to visit his apartment at night, he hadn't been up for camping out on the bare floor. Now it was Sam's fault that Dylan had been increasingly irritable all day. He was a guy who didn't function well on less than eight hours of sleep.

Sam opened the door. "Sorry, man. I was gearing up to ask Natalie out for The Big Date."

Dylan rolled his eyes. "Well, she's on duty right now. At least wait for her break."

Sam gave Dylan a stiff salute. "Yes, sir!"

"Mock me all you want, Bardin." Dylan walked past Sam into the bathroom. "This is a business—not a social club." He slammed the bathroom door shut.

Sam raised one eyebrow. Dylan seemed to be bugged by more than lack of sleep. The guy had been edgy for a couple of days now. Maybe he was having panic attacks about having shelled out so much cash on his new car. Or maybe Dylan was worried that Sam was going to blow it with Natalie and send the whole gang into an extended conniption fit.

Sam nodded to himself. Yeah. That was probably it. Dylan liked to play big brother to Natalie's little sister. But Sam had no intention of treating Natalie's feelings with anything but the lightest touch. As soon as Dylan realized that Sam wasn't just talking the talk, his

131

protective nature would stop spinning out of control.

Sam scanned the café for Natalie's long brown ponytail. Nope. Nope. Nothing. Where was she? He needed to execute his plan to ask her out before he lost his nerve. Where are you, Nat? He was hoping for some telepathic message.

A second later Sam heard a low humming sound coming from the storeroom. Aha! He took a couple of steps toward the storeroom, then stopped. Was this a huge mistake? In a period of less than seven days he had gone from noticing Natalie as a real live girl for the first time to deciding that he wanted to pursue her as if she were the love of his life. Sam closed his eyes, remembering the sensation of her lips against his. While they had kissed, Sam hadn't thought once of his father, his mother, or his brother. It wasn't until he had slipped into the houseboat and tried to go to sleep that the reality of his broken life had crept back into his consciousness.

The door of the storeroom swung open. "Sam!" Natalie sounded (not unpleasantly) surprised to see him. "When did you get here?"

An hour ago. I've been sitting on a crate in the alley trying to figure out exactly what I was going to say to you. "A few minutes ago."

"Oh." Natalie shook the bag of coffee beans she had retrieved from the storeroom. In a tight pair of faded Levi's shorts and a red baby tee, she looked as beautiful this morning as she had at the beach last night. "Well, I guess I better go, uh, do something with these." She started to walk past Sam.

He reached out and clasped her arm. "Last night was really . . ."

"Special?" Natalie supplied. "And sort of strange and scary and mind-boggling?"

Were those adjectives positive or negative? It was hard to say. "Yeah, all that."

Natalie glanced down at her toenails, which were sticking out of thong sandals and painted pale pink. "Maybe we should just pretend it never happened—"

No! "Do you want to go out tomorrow night?" he said quickly. "With me, I mean?" He needed at least twenty-four hours to figure out where he was going to take her.

Natalie smiled. "Sure. I'd love to."

Sam ran his hand softly down the length of her bare arm. "We'll take it slow, okay?"

Natalie nodded. "Slow is good."

Air rushed back into his lungs. "Great . . . I'll pick you up at eight o'clock."

"I'll be at my house," Natalie told him. "You convinced me to move back."

Sam grinned. "I guess we both benefited from our conversation last night. I feel better than I have in weeks."

Natalie touched his hand. "I'm glad."

Dylan appeared at Sam's side. "Natalie, table four has been waiting for their lattes for almost fifteen minutes."

Natalie handed Dylan the bag of coffee beans. "I'll get right on it, boss."

"Good." Dylan's mood obviously hadn't improved in the last five minutes.

As Natalie walked away Dylan turned to Sam. "Try not to look so satisfied with yourself. It's disgusting." He disappeared into the storeroom and banged the door shut.

Sam glanced at the door, then back at Natalie, who was now walking across the café with a large tray of lattes. He was going to prove to Dylan that he was good for Natalie. As long as Sam didn't make any major mistakes (such as forgetting to call Natalie or accidentally asking out another girl), eventually Dylan would see that Sam was a stable individual who deserved an all-American girl. And then everyone—especially Sam—would be happy.

At four o'clock in the afternoon Dylan walked into the alley behind the café, closed his eyes, and leaned his head against the brick wall. Had there been a longer day in the history of time? He doubted it. Dylan was working on a sum total of two hours of sleep, the cash register had jammed three times, and every time he turned around, he found himself admiring the way Natalie's hair shone under the café lights. He had finally told Jason to fix the register and ducked outside. He wouldn't be able to get his life put back together in five minutes, but at least he could start lining up the pieces.

"Dylan?" Natalie was standing in the fire door. "Can I pull up a crate?"

He shrugged. "Help yourself. I was just about to go inside."

"Don't go," she said.

"Fine. I'll stay." He couldn't resist—no matter how pathetic it was—the chance to steal even a few minutes alone with her.

Natalie let the door bang shut behind her. He watched her long legs as she walked through his line of vision and perched daintily on an old orange milk crate. "Are you okay?" she asked softly.

"Never been better," Dylan answered. Never been worse, he silently corrected himself.

"Come on, Dylan . . . it's obvious that something is bothering you."

Dylan ran his hands through his short, light brown hair. He plastered on the fake smile he used when dealing with customers who still hadn't figured out the difference between espresso and café au lait. "I don't know what you're talking about. I'm great."

"If you say so . . ." She was frowning, which caused these really cute tiny lines to form between her eyes.

"I hear you've got big plans tomorrow night," Dylan said. Stupid. Stupid. Stupid. He didn't want to talk about Sam and Natalie. He didn't want to *think* about Sam and Natalie. But the urge to stare at the scene of the wreck was too powerful to suppress.

Natalie blushed. "Did Sam, uh, tell you what happened?"

"Every detail." It wasn't his fault that Sam was the type to kiss and tell. Dylan wasn't going to lie for the guy.

"Oh." Natalie was bright red now. She crossed her

long legs and edged a little closer to him. "So what do you think?"

I think that I want to kiss you right now. "It's your life, Nat. Why do you care what I think?"

"Dylan!" Natalie sounded irritated, which was unusual in and of itself. "You know how much I value your opinion."

"We had the Great Pact for a reason," Dylan said. If she was going to insist on asking him questions, then she was going to have to deal with the answers—even if the answers were totally biased.

Natalie sighed. "I'm just so confused. . . . Sam is a great friend, but I've never thought of him like *that.*"

Dylan felt his mood lighten. "Really?"

Natalie nodded. "But just because I haven't seen him that way in the past doesn't mean I can't *now.* Right?"

He had to play this very carefully. Yeah, it was great that Natalie hadn't thought about Sam as a boyfriend before now. But she'd clearly never thought of Dylan that way, either. "I don't know, Nat."

"You sound so serious," Natalie said. "Is there some other reason why I shouldn't go out with Sam? Some reason that you don't want to tell me about?"

Dylan's heart actually hurt, it was beating so fast. He had to tell her the truth. He had to tell her now. "Natalie, I—"

"What?" She was leaning so close that he could see his reflection in the pupils of her beautiful hazel eyes.

"I . . ." He bent toward her. Natalie's lips were just millimeters away. If he moved his face just a fraction of an inch, they would be kissing.

Dylan jerked back. He couldn't. He just couldn't do it. Not to Sam. And not to her. "Nothing. There's no reason at all."

"I guess I'll just wait and see what happens," Natalie said quietly. "Maybe I'll know more about how I feel after tomorrow night."

"Maybe." Dylan's mood plunged again. He had been relegated to the position of confidante. He knew guys who were always stuck listening to the girl they were pining after blab on and on about their boyfriends. Those guys were pitiful.

"Can't you talk to Tanya about this stuff?" he asked.

"Sure." She grinned. "But you're an infinitely better listener."

Terrific. He was the sensitive nineties guy who would always lend an ear. What could be more unattractive than that? It was probably a good thing he hadn't worked up the guts to confess his feelings to Natalie before Sam swooped in with his macho moves. He would have faced serious humiliation, which would have been magnified by Sam's subsequent conquest.

Natalie stood up. "Thanks, Dylan." She patted his head and dropped a light kiss on his forehead. "I feel *much* better."

Dylan silently groaned. He didn't want Natalie to feel better. He wanted her to feel as desperately, miserably in love as he did.

Independently *Blue*:
Sara Jane O'Connor Contemplates a Life of Seclusion

I'm sick of people. When I was younger, my favorite thing to do was to hole up in my room and pretend that I was the only person alive on earth. I'd store bags of potato chips and two-liter bottles of Coke under my bed, guarding myself against possible invasion by aliens. Let me tell you this: I was never bored, and I was never irritated by the company I was keeping—me, myself, and I.

Then I started going to school and camp and stupid mixers. Slowly I bought into the adult bureaucracy that operated on the principle that no man (or girl) could exist in a social vacuum. So I got myself hopelessly entangled with various people and places, determined to do my part to fit into society at large.

For a while that was all fine. I allowed myself to be drawn into a situation that involved group dynamics and compromise. I went to parties, hung out, even told all my secrets to my so-called best friend.

But enough is enough. I'm ready to retreat to my bedroom and build an indestructible fort. People can be mean—even worse, they can't seem to stop themselves from being devious. In my fort I'll be alone. I may even be lonely.

But I'll be alone on my own terms—a precious commodity in a world based on constant disappointment and negotiation.

"I'm glad you called." Celia Dalton was leaning forward in her chair, which caused her rather low-cut blouse to be even more, er, low cut.

"Me too. I think." Jason picked up his fork, then put it down. He did the same with the knife. And the spoon.

Jason had convinced himself that Celia was right about her advice that he should find a girlfriend—or some facsimile thereof. He and Blue were never going to get back to the way they had been before Matthew Chance's party if all he could think about when he was with her was how much he wanted to kiss her soft, red lips. Maybe if he had someone else to kiss—someone else who was beautiful—he could transfer his feelings for Blue onto that new someone.

"I guess you thought a lot about what I said." Celia was also holding various pieces of silverware . . . but in a totally different way from Jason. She was sort of . . . caressing the tines of her fork.

"Guess so." Terrific conversation. He was a real charmer. Not that he cared about being charming.

Maybe this whole date—if it was

ELEVEN

a date—had been a huge mistake. All he could think about was Blue. Which is exactly why you're here, he reminded himself. He couldn't stand the way every time he looked at her all he could do was picture Blue in that pink tank top she had worn to his seventeenth birthday party dinner. So he had retrieved the scrap of paper on which Celia had written her number from the wicker wastebasket in his room and spent all of two hours working up the nerve to give her a call. After all, she was the only other girl he *knew,* much less one who had given him a number and an open invitation.

Now they were sitting across from each other at Arte Pasta. The last time Jason had been here, he and Blue had almost ended up having to wash dishes to pay for their meal. Neither one of them had thought very carefully before ordering salad *and* a dessert.

"Do you like me?" Celia asked. "Do you want to kiss me?"

Jason gulped. Danger! Danger! The yellow light had turned red. He was in *way* over his head. Dr. Grady! Help me! "Like, right now? Here?"

Celia laughed. "Let's start with, 'Do you want to kiss me in general?' Then we'll move on to when and where."

Jason was totally unprepared for the onslaught of sensations that assailed every cell of his body. No! Yes! No! Maybe! Yes! "I haven't really thought about it yet. . . . Kissing you, I mean."

140

"There's no time like the present." Celia's bare foot (apparently she had slipped off one of the high-heeled sandals she was wearing) was working its way up Jason's calf.

He sucked in a deep breath. Blue's face the night of Matthew Chance's party (and their non-date) flashed against the movie screen in his head. Bad thought. Totally, utterly wrong thought. "Sure. I mean, I'd be crazy not to want to kiss you . . . right?"

Celia slid her foot back into her sandal. "You tell me."

Why wasn't this restaurant equipped with oxygen tanks? "How's your summer been so far?" Jason asked. Okay, so he was making the lamest attempt of all time to change the subject. Who could blame him? Okay, so every red-blooded American guy in the world could blame him. . . .

"Jason?" Celia's voice was huskier than he remembered.

"Uh, yeah?" Had he responded out loud? Jason stared at Celia's dark red lips, mesmerized.

"Do you want to skip the dinner thing? It's sort of dull." She threw her napkin on her plate and pushed back her chair.

He wanted something about this night to be different. But Jason wasn't sure that dinner at Arte Pasta was the problem. "Sure, let's get out of here." He had pretty much lost his appetite, anyway.

141

"Awesome." As Celia stood up, Jason studied the dress she was wearing. The material was this sort of black satiny stuff, and it clung to her body in such a way that Jason was having a tough time not thinking about what Celia might look like underneath.

Blue would never wear a dress like that. She thought women in the nineties should rely on their personality—not their body—to make an impression. Jason had always agreed with Blue's philosophy. But staring at Celia, he couldn't help wondering what Blue herself would look like in a slinky, sexy outfit. Wait a second. The whole point of tonight was to *not* think of Blue in . . . that way.

Jason stood up and followed Celia to the front of the restaurant. In just seconds he was going to be faced with a dilemma. If he and Celia weren't going to have dinner, what *were* they going to do?

He stopped next to Celia at the entrance of Arte Pasta. She handed him her small leather jacket to help her into. Jason held out the coat awkwardly. He wasn't used to these male-female niceties. He had never so much as opened a door for Blue.

"Want to go back to my house?" Celia asked. "My parents let me convert the garage into a pretty cool place to hang out—it's sort of Brady Bunch meets Rupaul."

"Sure . . . we can listen to music or something."

Jason pushed the sleeves of Celia's jacket up to her shoulders. Hey, this wasn't bad.

"Or something." Celia flashed a suggestive (at least Jason interpreted it that way) grin.

Jason opened the door of Arte Pasta. Was he prepared for this? An actual make-out session seemed imminent. What exactly would be expected of him? And what was *he* supposed to expect from *her?* Don't panic. . . .

"Oomph!" Jason ran straight into a person who was trying to enter the restaurant. "Excuse me," he said automatically.

"Is that any way to greet an old friend?"

Jason's eyes practically bugged out of his head. He felt like a cartoon character.

It was Blue. Mr. and Mrs. O'Connor were standing behind her, staring somewhat disapprovingly at the shocked and confused expression on Jason's face. "What are you doing here?"

"I got held hostage by my parents. They're making me eat out in public with them or die." Blue shifted from one foot to the other, looking slightly uncomfortable. "What are *you* doing here?"

"Uh . . ." This was a tough one. He had accidentally on purpose forgotten to mention to Blue that he had asked Celia out on a date.

Celia gripped his elbow in a possessive gesture that Jason had seen on *Melrose Place* but never in real life. "He's with me," she coldly informed Blue.

143

"Oh." Blue's face was turning this really funny shade—something between pea green and jaundice yellow.

Mr. O'Connor stepped forward. "Come on, Sara Jane. There's a bowl of spaghetti and clam sauce with your name on it."

Blue didn't need to be told twice. She barreled past Jason and headed into the restaurant.

"I'll talk to you later, okay?" Jason called after her. Blue didn't respond. She just kept walking. Jason more or less stumbled out onto the sidewalk in front of Arte Pasta. What had just transpired?

Celia was still holding his elbow tightly. "Who was *that* girl?" she asked.

Jason gently pulled his arm out of her grip. Identifying Blue seemed like an enormous task. "That was Blue," he said simply.

Celia glanced back at the restaurant. "I thought her name was Sara Jane."

Jason nodded. "Blue is a nickname." He couldn't imagine someone encountering Blue and not even knowing who she was. To Jason, she represented the whole world.

"Don't tell me you're going to sulk all night because she blew you off," Celia said.

Jason was struck by the sheer force of Celia's personality. He had never met a girl (except Blue) who was so at ease with confrontation. "No. Definitely not."

Celia headed toward her black Jeep Cherokee, which was parked in front of Arte Pasta. She'd had to drive since Jason planned never to get behind the wheel of a car again. She stopped in front of the Jeep and leaned against the passenger side door. "You know, now that I've actually seen interaction between you and Blue, I'm more convinced than ever that you should follow my advice."

"Your advice?" When you don't know what to say, play dumb.

Celia reached for his hands. "Don't pretend like you don't remember."

Busted. "I need a girlfriend," Jason mumbled.

Celia's hands were soft and warm. Jason pulled her a little closer to him, his heart hammering in his chest.

Celia let go of his hands and slipped her arms around his neck. "Right. You need a girlfriend."

"Or something," Jason said softly. He thought briefly of Blue, then gave her image a mental shove to the back of his brain. He needed something different. And new.

Jason leaned forward, watching as Celia's lips came closer and closer. Finally he closed his eyes and brushed his mouth against hers. "Or something," Celia echoed.

Her arms tightened around his neck. Jason kissed her again, longer this time. "Now you're getting it," Celia whispered. Her voice was slow and throaty. She slipped out of his arms and headed toward the other side of the car.

Jason reached for the handle of the passenger

side door. Breathe in. Breathe out. Steady. As he slid into the car he glanced back at Arte Pasta one last time. Blue was standing in the restaurant window, her eyes hard and cold.

Jason sighed deeply. Was it possible that his efforts to repair his friendship with Blue were only going to cause more damage?

Blue stared out the large window of Arte Pasta. Jason and Celia were gone, but Blue couldn't seem to move her feet. The thought of eating a huge bowl of fettuccine was out of the question. So. That was the girl from Java Gaya. Blue hated her. She hated her with a passion almost matched by her hatred for Craig.

Jason had acted as if he barely knew Blue. It was like they were acquaintances—not best friends. And the way Celia had been clutching Jason's hand . . . it was positively revolting. Blue didn't even want to think about the spit swap she had just witnessed. She thought PDA had gone out of style in the late eighties.

"Sara Jane, our table's ready." Mr. O'Connor's voice boomed in her ear.

Blue forced herself to look away from the window. "Great."

She followed her parents across the small restaurant. Where had Jason and Celia been going? Were they planning to make out all night, or was actual conversation going on between them? And which possibility actually bothered her more?

"Sara Jane, I asked you a question." Mrs. O'Connor was looking at Blue as if she was worried that her daughter was on some kind of drug trip.

"Sorry . . . what?" Stay here, Blue told herself. Don't think about *them*.

"I asked you how long Jason had been dating his . . . friend."

"They're not *dating*," Blue snapped.

"Let's order," Mr. O'Connor declared.

"Good idea." Blue didn't want to waste one more breath on discussing Jason Kirk. Or his kissing partner.

She had realized Saturday morning that she was in no way, shape, or form in love with Jason. Her feelings, to the contrary, had been caused by a brief break with reality. And even if she had decided she *did* love Jason in *that* way, it obviously wouldn't have mattered. Jason wanted a girlfriend like Celia—someone sexy and aggressive. He would never see Blue as anything more than a buddy to hang out with at the arcade.

And from this moment forward Blue would forget those three small words he had murmured the night of the party. Yep. Jason could do whatever stupid thing he wanted to . . . and it wouldn't bother her one bit.

"Nice apartment," Tanya commented. Actually the place was incredibly run-down and entirely too small to fit three inhabitants. But Tanya wasn't sure what else she was supposed to say. This whole night had been an entirely new experience for her. Major had picked her up at home (where he had charmed her mother into a pool of melted butter). Then they had gone to a jazz concert in Golden Gate Park, where Major had caught Tanya completely and totally off guard by presenting her with a picnic basket (okay, a paper bag) full of cheese, crackers, fruit, and sparkling water. For exactly ninety-one minutes Tanya and Major had sat so close to each other that Tanya's hand had grazed Major's thigh every time she reached for a cracker. But not once had he kissed her. Not one lousy time.

By the end of the concert Tanya had convinced herself that Major thought she was a total dog. After all, what self-respecting male didn't try to kiss a girl when the night was dark, the music romantic, and the moon full? But then he had asked her back to his place for coffee. And she had nodded without even trying to play hard to get. This guy was way more than she could handle. Exponentially more.

Major grinned. "Don't worry. I know the apartment is a hole."

"Well, it could use a little . . . redecorating." She glanced around the living room, which was possibly the most masculine space she had ever encountered in her life.

The room had at some point been painted white—now it was a dingy shade of gray. There were two couches, both of which were plaid and upholstered with some sort of material that looked as if it would give a person a nasty rash. And there were tattered posters of rock stars and athletes mounted (seemingly arbitrarily) on the walls. Most of the scratched wood floor was covered with a faded orange shag carpet that had probably been retrieved from someone's parents' rec room. Tanya's gaze drifted down the hall, where she assumed the bedrooms were.

Major took a step closer to her in that incredibly disconcerting way he had. "Want to see the rest of the place?" he asked softly.

"What about the cup of coffee you promised me?" she asked.

"Caffeine is the last thing I need right now," Major said. His voice was full of the promise of . . . what? "Do you want a tour or not?"

Breathe, Tanya, breathe. "Uh, sure." She was brutally aware of the smell of him—Ivory soap had never had a better advertisement.

Tanya followed Major down the bare, narrow hallway. The door of the first room was wide open. A carpet of dirty clothes, waterlogged magazines, and broken CD cases covered the floor. A smell that Tanya had always associated with guys' locker rooms emanated from the depths of the messy (understatement of the year) room.

"Are any of your, uh, roommates home?" Tanya asked. They seemed so completely alone. . . . It was like anything (and she did mean anything) could happen in the sanctity of the empty apartment.

"Chris is at his girlfriend's for the night, and Jake is house-sitting for his parents' dogs—his folks are at a corporate retreat in Hawaii." Major stopped in front of another room. The door was shut tight, and a Do Not Disturb sign was hanging from the knob. "Why do you want to know?" Major asked.

He put his arms around Tanya's waist and pulled her close to him. *Breathe.* "I was just, uh, curious. . . ."

"Are you scared?" Major's dark eyes seemed to be looking straight into her brain.

"No!" Tanya yelped. Yes. I'm scared of you. . . . I'm scared of me. I'm afraid of this empty apartment. "Like I said, I was just curious."

"I don't bite," Major said softly. "Unless, of course, you want me to. . . ."

"Is this your room?" Tanya's voice was high and shrill. She felt like a seventh-grader in the midst of an intense game of spin the bottle.

Major nodded. "This is it, babe." He opened the door of the room.

Tanya peered into the room. It was like something from the Citadel. In the middle of the room there was a neatly made double bed (complete with an ultramasculine navy blue comforter). An oak desk faced the room's one large window. Every book, paper, and pen was stacked with a precision that Tanya could barely fathom. The white walls were blank except for a poster of Martin Luther King Jr.

"Are you involved in some kind of anal-retentive contest?" Tanya asked. "This place looks like a hospital room."

Major laughed. "I like to keep my life neat—everything in its place."

He closed the door to the room and walked back toward the living room. Tanya followed him. "Does that go for *everything* in your life—or just your room?"

Major turned around to face her. "Everything. I'm not going to let anything deter me from the Grand Plan."

Tanya nodded. "Where do I fit into the Grand Plan?"

Major slipped his arms around her waist. "You don't, Tanya. . . . That's the problem."

There was this feeling in Tanya's heart. She felt like either an ice pick or a king-size Swiss Army knife had plunged through her aorta. "What are you saying?"

Major's arms tightened around her. "I like you, Tanya." His lips brushed the nape of her neck, sending shivers down her spine straight to her red-painted toenails. "Maybe I like you too much."

She forced herself to concentrate on Major's words rather than the way his lips kept grazing across the soft skin between her shoulder blades. "I don't . . . understand."

"I wasn't playing hard to get when I told you that I'm not looking for a relationship right now."

"But what if you found one?" she asked. Tanya hoped that her voice sounded as casual and indifferent as she wanted it to.

Major stared into her eyes. "I'm not *going* to find one, Tanya. . . . I want you to know that now."

Tanya raised her eyebrows, putting on her Power Girl face. "FYI, I don't want to get involved, either. . . . I just want to have a good time." Liar!

"If I believed that were true, then I wouldn't feel so guilty when I do this. . . ." He bent his head and captured her lips with his.

Tanya leaned against him, circling his neck with her hands. The kiss washed over her, blocking out any common sense that she had managed to hang on to around Major. He broke away from her. "Can you handle it? Can you handle *us?*"

Proceed with caution. Above all else, she had to protect herself. Because dating Major was heartbreak waiting to happen. If she had any brains whatsoever, she would turn around, walk away, and never look back. Luckily she *didn't* have any brains.

"Kiss me," Tanya whispered. She closed her eyes and surrendered herself to the feel of Major's lips on hers. She would worry about the state of her heart *after* she made out with Major for about fifty years.

Chef Natalie Presents a Dish for All You Vegetarians Out There

I haven't always been a huge zucchini fan, but lately I've learned to appreciate its fresh, crunchy taste. That said, I hope you enjoy this simple but elegant dish that will enhance any meal.

Zucchini Parmesan

Ingredients:
- 4- to 5-inch zucchini
- 2 tablespoons vegetable oil
- 4 tablespoons butter
- 1/4-pound Parmesan cheese, grated

Directions:
Preheat oven to 350 degrees. Add zucchini and oil to a 4-quart pan of boiling water; parboil 10 minutes. Remove and drain.

Cut zucchini in half lengthwise. Place cut side up in a buttered 9 x 13–inch baking dish, season with salt and pepper, dot with butter. Cover with cheese.

Bake 15 minutes or until heated through. Before serving lightly brown cheese under preheated boiler.

Makes 6 to 8 servings.

Present the dish to your friends or family with a flourish, then sit back and enjoy the praise that comes pouring in. You deserve it!

Rage was a relatively new sensation for Blue. Sure, she had been angry at her brother and her parents plenty of times in the past. And yes, there had been times when she would've gladly punched Tanya and/or Natalie in the nose if such behavior was socially acceptable. There had even been a couple of occasions when she'd had to clench her teeth to keep herself from biting Jason's head off with a sarcastic, pointed remark. But this full-out self-righteous fury was totally exhausting.

After dinner at Arte Pasta, Blue had revised her opinion of Jason. True, he could do whatever he wanted *with* whomever he wanted. But he didn't have the right to treat her as if she didn't exist. She deserved at least a modicum of respect. After all, the last *she* had been informed, she was the guy's best friend. Yeah, right. Obviously he had just been passing time with Blue until something more . . . enticing . . . came along.

It was Wednesday afternoon, and Blue had successfully avoided speaking to Jason for the past three hours. At this rate she was quite

TWELVE

sure she could maintain the silent treatment for a good thirty or forty years before she cracked. Out of the corner of her eye Blue saw Jason standing by the cappuccino maker. He smiled and gestured her to come over to him. Instead Blue did a one-eighty and sank into a chair next to Natalie.

"What's up?" Natalie asked. She was staring at the monitor of the Gateway 2000.

Blue shrugged. "Besides the sky, absolutely nothing."

Natalie clicked the mouse and entered a chat room about organic food. "You're perky," she commented.

"Just so you know, I'm staging a one-woman crusade against friendship . . . so don't be offended if I stop talking to you."

Natalie turned away from the monitor, the inevitable look of concern in her hazel eyes. "Did something happen between you and Jason?"

"No." Far from it. Jason had simply decided to cut her out of his life without so much as a thank-you note.

"I don't believe you," Natalie said. "He's walking around pouting like a member of Heaven's Gate who got left behind on Earth. And you're planning to defect from society." She pointed to her head. "I may not belong to Mensa, but it doesn't take a genius to figure out that you two are suffering from some kind of meltdown."

Why did Natalie have to be so perceptive?

The girl was a walking pop-psychology pamphlet. "Let's just say there's a failure to communicate."

Natalie was staring back at the computer screen. Her eyes were sort of glazed over, and she didn't even seem to be listening to Blue. Great. "Nat? Hello?"

"This is so weird . . . ," Natalie said softly. "Total déjà vu."

"What?" Blue leaned forward so that she could get a better view of the computer screen. Natalie wasn't a girl who tended to tune out of a conversation when she was trying to pry out a piece of personal information.

On one side of the monitor there was a large color graphic that diagrammed how best to plant the seeds in an organic vegetable garden. On the other side of the screen there was a column about the benefits of a vegan diet.

Natalie was still staring at the screen. "What's got you so freaked?" Blue asked again.

Natalie shook her head. "It's nothing. . . . The woman who wrote that column has the same name my mom did. Her maiden name, I mean." She pointed to the article byline. *Delia Broderick* was written in small, eight-point type.

"Wow," Blue said. "It seems like a pretty uncommon name."

Natalie nodded. "I know." She clicked the mouse again. "I'm going to send Delia Broderick an E-mail. Maybe she's some kind of long lost relative."

"Maybe so." Blue shoved her chair back as Natalie began to compose what Blue suspected would be a very long E-mail.

She felt Jason's eyes on her as she stood up. Any other time Blue would have walked over to him and made a joke about organic farms. Or confided that Natalie had tried to get Blue to "open up" for the umpteenth time that week. She would have suggested that they ditch work for half an hour and go play pinball at Arthur's Bar & Grill across the street. But not today.

Blue refused to look in Jason's direction. Instead she headed for the door. Jason was useless. But she could still go play Spy Hunter. Alone.

"Home again, home again," Jason greeted his psychiatrist, Dr. Grady. "It seems like I was just here yesterday."

Jason had been visiting his psychiatrist once a week, every week, since he had been released from Turner House a couple of years ago. At the time he had been depressed and suicidal. Jason had worked his way up to being just the depressed part, but his parents still insisted that he see Dr. Grady. At this point Jason felt as if his brain was a laboratory in which Dr. Grady was conducting some endless experiment.

"You're talkative today," Dr. Grady commented. He peered at Jason over his ever present horn-rimmed glasses.

Jason clamped his mouth shut. He tried to co-operate as little as possible with Dr. Grady's con-stant probing into the inner workings of his subconscious. He collapsed into the black leather chair opposite Dr. Grady's and waited for the shrink to ask him a question.

"What's new?" Dr. Grady asked. The question was number five on his rotating list of ten opening lines.

"I went on a date," Jason said. "Actually I went on two dates . . . sort of. The first one, which I told you about last week, turned out to be with Blue, who I like totally wouldn't go out with. . . ." He took a deep breath. "But the second date was with this really wacky girl who I met at this coffee shop . . . and it was actually sort of fun."

Jason sat back and waited for the praise to come. Dr. Grady had been badgering him to ex-plore his so-called emotional side for months now.

"Wonderful," Dr. Grady proclaimed. "Tell me about it."

"We went to dinner. . . . Well, actually we didn't go to dinner. . . ." Jason's mind flashed to the image of Blue standing in the window of Arte Pasta. "We ran into Blue, actually."

"Hmmm . . . interesting." Dr. Grady tapped his fingers together and gave Jason one of his patented

I-think-this-could-be-breakthrough-material looks.

"Yeah. I didn't tell her I was going on the date or anything . . . and I guess it kind of hurt her feelings."

"I see." Dr. Grady leaned forward in his chair. "How does that make you feel? Hurting Blue's feelings?"

"Terrible. Horrible." There was an actual lump in Jason's throat. Dr. Grady was always trying to get him to start bawling, and for the first time Jason felt that a tear rolling down his cheek might be imminent. "She wouldn't even talk to me at the café today."

"Why do you think her feelings were hurt?" Dr. Grady asked. "Let's explore that."

Jason shrugged. "I guess 'cause I didn't tell her I had asked this girl out . . . and we usually tell each other *everything.*"

"Do you think Blue might be in love with you?" Dr. Grady asked. "And is it possible that you're in love with her, too?"

Jason's stomach dropped to his feet. He couldn't allow himself to contemplate those questions. "No!" he shouted.

Dr. Grady nodded. "Okay . . . then what *are* your feelings for each other?"

"We're *friends,*" Jason snapped. "I've told you that, like, five million billion times."

"This subject seems to make you very uncomfortable," Dr. Grady commented. He picked up the legal pad sitting on the table next to his chair and made a note.

Jason hated it when Dr. Grady made notes. It made him feel like he was getting demerits. Enough demerits and he'd wind up in detention (which, in this case, consisted of the loony bin). Jason needed to change the topic of conversation—pronto.

"I was in a car with a girl for the first time since the incident," Jason blurted.

Dr. Grady settled more deeply into his seat. "Wonderful. How did that make you feel?"

"Weird." Jason hadn't expected ever to drive in a car with a girl again.

The night of his accident he had been with a girl. Ellie Twyman had been riding shotgun in the Jeep his parents had bought him for his sixteenth birthday. Jason had been on top of the world . . . and determined to impress Ellie. So determined that he had been paying less than no attention to the road.

"What are you thinking about right now?" Dr. Grady asked.

Jason closed his eyes. There had been a crash. He hadn't been looking at the street, and suddenly he had heard a loud thump against the hood of the Jeep. "Tires squealing. Glass breaking. That sound . . . the crying."

"Whose crying?" Dr. Grady pressed.

"Her's . . . Ellie's."

"Was anyone else crying?" Dr. Grady was practically out of his seat now. He had been urging

Jason to talk about this stuff forever. But Jason usually refused to say more than a word or two about the accident that had led to his mental breakdown.

"Me," Jason admitted. "I was crying. . . . I knew he was dead. I knew the little boy was dead."

Jason ignored the tear that was sliding down his cheek. Now he remembered the real reason he could never be with Blue. He didn't deserve her. He was scum. He was worse than scum. He was a murderer.

"He hasn't called me," Tanya whined. "Why hasn't he called me?"

Natalie rolled her eyes. Tanya, Queen of Melodrama, was out in full force. It was late Wednesday afternoon, and Blue, Tanya, and Natalie were taking an extended coffee break. They had claimed the booth for themselves an hour ago—so far the girls had inhaled three mugs of coffee, three doughnuts, and two strawberry tarts.

"Your date was *last night*," Natalie reminded Tanya. "It's been less than twenty-four hours since you guys spoke."

Tanya slumped in the booth and rested her forehead on the table. "I'm never going to see him again. I know it."

Blue swallowed a bite of her strawberry tart. "This is exactly why I shun all things having to do

162

with romance."

"But he's *so* amazing," Tanya said. She sat back up in the booth. A blue Equal wrapper was stuck to her forehead. "I don't think I can live without him." She sighed dramatically. "How come the one guy I want isn't interested in having a relationship with me?"

Natalie laughed. "T., you've never met a guy you couldn't live without. Major is no different."

"I guess. . . ." Tanya's eyes were soft and far away. Natalie wondered if her own eyes looked that way when she thought about Sam. Probably not. At least not yet.

"You're actually making some sense, Nat," Blue said. "Don't tell me you're finally through with your Matthew Chance obsession."

"She's moved on," Tanya said. "Natalie has a date tonight."

"With whom?" Blue asked. "And how come nobody ever tells me what's going on around here?"

"They probably don't tell you because they know you'll criticize them if they do anything that doesn't jive with your philosophy of the world at large," Natalie commented. She, for one, was tired of hearing Blue talk about how everyone on earth except her was totally stupid.

"Her date is with Sam," Tanya stage-whispered.

"Sam who?" Blue asked.

"Sam Bardin," Tanya said.

"Let's just broadcast the news to all of San Francisco," Natalie snapped. She was suddenly

163

feeling acutely aware of everyone in the café who might be in a position to overhear their conversation.

Blue was staring at Natalie. "This is a joke, right?"

Natalie shook her head. "It's true." There was no point in trying to keep this a secret. Between her and Sam, the entire staff of @café already knew that they had kissed the other night.

"You guys are friends!" Blue shouted. "You're going to ruin everything!"

Tanya arched one eyebrow. "Well, someone is sure hot and bothered."

Natalie grinned. "Do you think she's *projecting?*" she asked Tanya. The temptation to tease Blue was too great to ignore. Anyone with half a brain could see that the girl was crazy in love with Jason.

"Shut up," Blue snapped. "Please." She picked up her coffee and slurped loudly.

"Do you think I should call Major?" Tanya asked no one in particular.

"I'm not even sure I like Sam that way," Natalie said. "I mean, I *think* I do . . . but how can I be sure?"

"Jason really is a jerk," Blue said. "I couldn't care less who he wants to waste his time with, but I don't understand why he feels like he has to act like a little date is some huge *secret.*"

"I'm *not* going to call him," Tanya declared. "In fact, I'm never going to see Major again. . . . He's not worth all this hassle."

Natalie leaned back in the booth and closed her eyes. This conversation was going in circles.

"Getting involved with Sam is going to be a huge mistake," Blue said to Natalie. Apparently she had emerged from her Jason trance.

"You never know until you know," Tanya said. "On the other hand, I *know* that Major and I are doomed." She sighed deeply. "But you don't *know* that you and Sam won't be heading down the aisle together in a few years—I say go for it."

Natalie needed to take an Advil. Maybe two. Why was it that everyone—with the major exception of herself—knew what was right for her?

From: Jasonk443
To: BlueladyCC:
Subject: Why aren't you speaking to me?

Blue,

    Since you refuse to speak to me, I have to resort to electronic communication. I don't know why you're so mad at me, but how can we fix it if you won't *talk* to me?

• • • • • • • • • • • • • • •

From: Bluelady
To: Jasonk443 CC:
Subject: Re: Why aren't you speaking to me?

Jason:

    If you don't know why I'm mad, then I'm not going to tell you.

• • • • • • • • • • • • • • •

From: Jasonk443
To: BlueladyCC:
Subject: This is totally stupid

Blue,

    Give me a break, please! You're being totally unreasonable. As far as I can tell, you're mad because I went out with Celia without telling you about it. . . . The only reason I didn't tell you was because I knew you would disapprove. How's that for knowing why you're mad?

• • • • • • • • • • • • • • •

From: Bluelady
To: Jasonk443CC:
Subject: Re: This is totally stupid

Jason,

    Fine. Consider me officially not mad. Happy?

Sam stopped his motorcycle in front of the houseboat. He got off the front of the bike, then extended his hand to Natalie. "I'm sorry about this, Nat."

Natalie placed her hand gently in his and slid off the back of the bike. "Don't worry about it, Sam. Really."

"You're the best, Natalie." Sam kept her hand in his as they started up the dock that led to the houseboat.

This wasn't exactly what he had planned for their first date. The evening had started off without any major glitches. They had gone to Electra for dinner and made it through their entrées with a smattering of pleasant conversation and mild laughter. Unfortunately Eddie had called the restaurant halfway through the dessert and begged Sam to come home. Apparently Mrs. Bardin was crying uncontrollably. Sam had offered to drop Natalie off at home, but she had insisted on coming along and braving Sam's emotional baggage.

Eddie opened the door of the houseboat as they neared the end of the dock. "She's asleep," he announced.

Thank you, God. "Is she okay?" Sam asked.

Eddie shrugged. "For now."

THIRTEEN

"What happened?" Sam asked. "Did she freak out or what?"

Eddie bit his lip. He looked dangerously close to tears himself. "We were eating dinner—I made grilled cheese sandwiches for us. And she started talking about how things used to be. . . ."

"Uh-oh. I know where that leads." Sam dreaded the moments when his mother began to wax poetic about their old house, old schools, and old life, period.

Natalie let go of Sam's hand and put her arm around Eddie's shoulders. "It's a good thing you were here," she told him. "I'm sure you were a big help."

Typical Natalie. She always knew just what to say. Sam probably would have given Eddie a punch on the arm and told him to try to pretend that the whole thing never happened.

"I better check on her," Sam said. But he didn't make a move toward the hallway that led to his mom's bedroom. The thought of looking at her swollen, tear-stained face made his stomach turn. Kids simply weren't supposed to be put in this position. It wasn't natural.

Natalie stepped toward Sam. She brushed his cheek with the back of her hand. "I'll go," she said. "I'll make sure she's tucked in."

Relief flooded through Sam. "Thanks, Nat. Again."

She smiled. "I'm happy to do it."

Sam slipped his arm around her waist. "Maybe we can still catch a movie later."

Natalie shook her head. "Let's just hang out

here." She glanced at Eddie. "We should probably stick around."

Had a more giving, understanding girl ever existed on the face of the planet? Natalie was manna from heaven. "I'll put together some sundaes," Sam offered. "For *all* of us."

Eddie's face lit up. "We can eat them up on the deck," he said. "It'll be great!"

"Perfect," Natalie said. She gave Sam a quick kiss on the cheek and headed inside.

"Her room is the last door on the right," Sam called after her.

He watched as Natalie walked quickly through the houseboat. The bright red of her long, bare sundress looked almost out of place. The atmosphere around the boat had become permanently drab.

"You're lucky, Sam," Eddie said. "I'd give anything to have a girl like that."

Sam nodded. He knew he wanted Natalie. Not like he'd wanted other girls—with an almost mindless passion and obsession—but with the certainty that he was making a good decision. Natalie's soothing manner and generous nature more than made up for any lack of sparks. If he knew what was good for him, Sam would hang on to Natalie forever.

Natalie climbed up the tiny staircase that led to the top deck of the houseboat. Tonight certainly wasn't turning out the way she expected. Sam's mother had been passed out on top of her bed, wearing slippers and a robe. Natalie had taken off the slippers and maneuvered Mrs. Bardin so that she was under the flowered comforter on her bed.

In her sleep she was beautiful and peaceful. It was hard for Natalie to imagine a woman like her sobbing in the arms of her youngest son. Staring down at Mrs. Bardin, Natalie had felt a familiar pang of longing for her own mother.

Natalie climbed the last rung of the ladder and hoisted herself on deck. "Hey, there," she said to Sam. "Where's Eddie?"

"He decided to play video games in his room. . . . He thought we might want to be alone."

Natalie sat down on the lounge chair next to Sam's. She wasn't sure how to respond to that statement. This whole night had been crazy. Dinner had seemed like such an official first date—as if Sam and Natalie had been meeting each other for the first time. But now that they were back at the houseboat, the dynamic had changed. They were just Sam and Nat, two old friends who happened to be passing an evening together.

"Your mom is fine," Natalie said. "She was probably just really tired. . . . Being under this kind of pressure must be mentally exhausting."

"It is," Sam agreed. "For all of us."

Natalie looked out at the Pacific Ocean. The stress that Sam was under was layered in the texture of his voice. The Sam she had known for so many years would never end a date by taking a girl home to make sure his mother was safe in bed. He wouldn't have taken a girl home at all. Sam had always kept people at a distance. She sensed that even his brother was just getting to know him. His isolation touched her deep inside.

She knew that kind of pain. She had known it since the day her father had announced that her mom had died and gone to heaven. Natalie's whole world had been blown apart. One minute Natalie had been a toddler, listening to her mother sing lullabies at night. The next day she had been a little girl without the comfort of a mother's arms. More than anything Natalie wished she could remember her mom more clearly. She had an impression of her, but it was fuzzy and vague. Everything about Delia van Lenton was now shrouded in permanent mystery.

"It's beautiful out here tonight," Natalie said. She didn't want to spend the next hour pining for a mother she could never have. And the night *was* gorgeous. There was a cool breeze, and the stars were almost as bright as they had been at the beach Sam took her to.

Sam didn't appear to be listening. "I don't know what I'm going to do about her," he said quietly. "How can I act as a parent to my own mother?"

Natalie scooted her chair closer to Sam's. "I have faith in you," she told him. "Everything will work out—I promise."

Sam shifted in his chair so that he was looking into her eyes. "You're always so serene . . . so calm. How do you do it?"

Natalie laughed. "I think you're talking about someone else." Was she uptight, worried, and overly aware of her surroundings at all times? Yes. Was she the Mona Lisa come to life? A big resounding no. "Dylan thinks I'm completely off my rocker."

Sam shook his head. "Dylan doesn't know what he's talking about. I mean, the way you just waltzed right in and handled everything . . . how can I thank you enough?"

"We're friends, Sam." She reached out and clasped his hand, a gesture that had become increasingly familiar to her during the past week. "Friends do those kinds of things for each other— no questions asked."

"Is that all we are?" he asked in a gravelly voice that she had overheard him use with girls in his days of womanizing. "Friends?"

Thank goodness for the cover of darkness. Natalie's face was probably turning the same color as her dress. "I don't know. . . ."

"Tell me what you're thinking, Natalie." Sam's voice was quietly insistent.

What *was* she thinking? For the past two days Natalie had thought of nothing but the kiss she and Sam had shared at the beach. She had enjoyed the feel of his lips, the smell of his hair, the softness of his hands as they had lightly brushed across her collarbone. But since Monday night she hadn't been obsessed with thinking about every detail of *Sam*. She had been obsessed with thinking about the ramifications of those kisses.

She didn't feel about Sam the way she had about Matthew, for instance. Or Dylan. When Natalie had been in love with Dylan, she had studied every detail about him—his personality, his face, his mannerisms. Sam didn't consume her every waking thought. He was more of a warm glow in the back of her mind. But she did love him. And he *was* one of the most attractive guys she had ever known. . . .

"Natalie?" Sam prompted. "Please, tell me how you feel."

Confused. Happy. Scared. "It's complicated," Natalie answered. It was the best she could do.

Sam leaned close. "Maybe this will make it a little simpler." He closed the rest of the distance between them, lightly kissing her on the lips.

A shiver of pleasure ran up Natalie's spine. She liked kissing—she liked it very much.

"And this," Sam whispered. He kissed her again, longer this time.

Natalie moved in her chair so that their bodies were almost touching. Relationships were complicated, but Sam was right. Kissing was very, very simple. "I like this," Natalie told him.

Sam grinned. "I like *you.*"

Natalie closed her eyes and waited for the next kiss. If she wasn't mistaken, she had just landed herself a boyfriend. A real, live boyfriend. *Her search was over.*

"Stop me, Dylan." Tanya was sitting on a stool at the café's bar, staring out into the night.

"Stop you from what?" He followed her gaze but didn't see anything on the sidewalk outside that was out of the ordinary.

"Stop me from myself." Tanya slouched so low on the stool that her chin was just inches away from the countertop. Even her curls looked a little limp.

"Jeez, T. This sounds dire."

Tanya groaned. "It is."

He and Tanya were a perfect pair, at least tonight. They were both miserable. "Do you want to talk about it?" Dylan asked.

Usually he wasn't overly interested in listening to Tanya's never ending litany of personal problems. But at the moment he would welcome any distraction. For the past several hours he had done nothing but picture Sam and Natalie engaged in a heavy-duty make-out session. The mental image, combined with four cups of coffee, was turning his stomach into one big ulcer waiting to happen.

"I don't *want* to." Tanya groaned. "But if I don't, I'm afraid I'm going to do something really, really stupid."

Dylan glanced around the café. The place had been empty for almost an hour. He and Tanya were just killing time by hanging around here. "Let's go to my place," he said. "We can hang out and discuss everything that's wrong with the world."

Tanya slid off the stool. "Sounds good. Just don't offer me a cup of coffee. I passed my limit three espressos ago."

174

Dylan laughed. "Herbal tea all the way."

Dylan walked around the café, turning off every light and the various coffeemakers behind the counter. He lived in constant fear of fire. Insurance was a luxury he couldn't afford.

Tanya locked the cash register. "How come you're being so nice, anyway?"

"I have my reasons." He wasn't about to reveal the fact that he was in love with her best friend—no matter how badly he wanted to confess to someone.

Tanya slipped on her black leather jacket. They walked outside in silence. "Good night, café," Dylan said as he did every night. He locked the door and tucked the key in the pocket of his Levi's.

"So, we're off to Casa Dylan," Tanya said.

"Yep." Dylan's studio apartment was only a couple of blocks from the café. They started walking down the street. "Are you going to tell me what I'm stopping you from or not?"

Tanya shrugged. "Do you want the truth or something a little prettier?"

"The truth would be nice."

"I'm trying not to get caught up in the whole Major thing," she said. "I mean, the guy is totally not interested in falling in love with me. Or with anyone else, for that matter."

"Uh-huh." He could relate to Major. Dylan wished to God that he hadn't fallen in love with Natalie.

"In this situation my first instinct is to run straight into the arms of some other available guy. I just want to make out like crazy and forget all about Major."

"I see. . . ." Dylan wasn't sure what to say. He wasn't entirely convinced that Tanya's solution was a bad one. Making out with someone sounded pretty good to him. Great, actually.

"But I'm trying to change my ways," Tanya said. "See, I did a really bad thing a couple of weeks ago. . . ."

"What?" Dylan asked. They reached the end of the block and turned left onto his street. He had a feeling that Tanya's confession was going to be a good one.

"I fooled around with Matthew Chance," Tanya said in a rush. "Please, please, don't hate me."

"I don't hate you." Dylan was too conflicted to hate anyone. "You're just *you*, Tanya. I don't think you can help yourself from doing the stuff you do."

"But you would never do something like that," Tanya said. "You would never fool around with the girl your best friend was in love with."

Two weeks ago he would have been able to answer that question in a heartbeat. Now he wasn't so sure. "I don't know what I'm capable of," Dylan admitted. "Who does?"

Actually Dylan was glad that Tanya had fooled around with Matthew. It made him feel less guilty about wishing Natalie the worst as far as her budding relationship with Sam was concerned. At least *someone* was a worse friend than he was.

"Do you feel like fooling around with someone now?" Tanya asked. Her voice had that *tone*. That

Tanya tone that made his blood run a little hotter.

"No," he lied. As sexy as Tanya was, Dylan didn't want to kiss anyone but Natalie.

"Liar." Tanya skipped up the front steps of his apartment building and waited for him at the top of the stairs.

Don't say anything. You'll regret it. You'll totally and completely regret it. "I'm sort of interested in someone else." He didn't need to give her any details. She had all the information she needed.

"Who?" Tanya asked. She sounded as surprised as if he had just told her he was secretly a multimillionaire.

"Just . . . someone." Man, he had forgotten how incredibly nosy Tanya was. The girl didn't like to have secrets kept from her—even if she was the master at having her own.

"Do I know her?" Tanya was sounding increasingly curious—not a good sign.

"Uh, yeah." Why wasn't he a better liar?

Tanya grabbed his arm. "Dylan, you do realize that I'm not going to quit bugging you until I find out who you're interested in." It was a statement, not a question.

He was toast. Burnt toast. "And if you don't tell me, I'll just ask around until I find someone who will," Tanya continued. "I'm sure Natalie has a clue who this mystery girl might be. Or Sam. Or Blue."

Dylan's heart was palpitating. Tanya could *not* go to Natalie and Sam with questions about Dylan's love interest. He had no choice. He had to tell her the truth and then throw himself at her mercy. If she had any heart at all, she would keep the information to herself.

"It's Natalie," Dylan said. "I'm in love with her."

Tanya's eyes widened. Actually they sort of popped out of her head. "No way!" she shouted. "You're joking."

Dylan nodded. He wondered if the degree of his misery showed on his face. "I wish I were."

Tanya's eyes were still bugging out of her head. "This is truly unbelievable."

"I know." Dylan felt closer to tears than he had since the time Sinjun McGuiness had stolen his bike in second grade. "I'm a total idiot."

"This is classic!" He'd known Tanya would have a dramatic reaction, but this was getting out of control. "Two best friends in love with the same girl. We're talking Shakespearean tragedy here, Dylan."

"Shut up." Dylan dug his keys out of his pocket. He had just made a huge mistake. He knew it. Dumb. Dumb. Dumb.

Tanya put her hand softly on his shoulder. "I think that's great, Dylan." Tanya sounded almost . . . sincere. "I mean, there's no reason why you *shouldn't* be in love with her."

"Really?" Maybe he hadn't made a mistake after all. Maybe Tanya could give him some advice. After all, if anyone knew how to get what she wanted, it was Tanya. "What about the fact that she just started dating my best friend . . . you know, the Shakespearean tragedy aspect?"

Tanya was nodding. "The idea of you and Natalie together—especially right now—*is* a little crazy. But it also makes a weird kind of sense."

Dylan opened the front door of the apartment building. "Thanks, T. That means a lot to me."

She hadn't told him to drop everything, search for Natalie, and declare his love on the spot. But she hadn't laughed in his face, either. And Tanya had never had a problem with hurting his feelings.

Tanya headed for the stairs. "Let's make some herbal tea and talk about your situation. This is way better than sitting around obsessing about Major."

Dylan followed Tanya up the stairs. This was going to be a long night. A very long, very interesting night. But before he and Tanya talked about Natalie, he had one very important task to complete. He had to swear her to secrecy.

He was just glad that Tanya had dropped the bombshell about herself and Matthew Chance. That particular tidbit of gossip gave him ammunition that should guarantee she would keep her mouth shut.

"Tanya?" he said softly.

She stopped midstep and turned around. "I know," she said. "I won't tell yours as long as you don't tell mine."

Dylan sighed with relief. His secret was safe. At least for now.

Tanya Childes Offers
Tori Spelling a Piece of Advice:
Get a Life!

Dear Tori,

I love you on *Beverly Hills 90210*. I mean, Donna Martin is a girl we can all look up to. She held on to her virginity longer than most modern girls (until she was over the age of twenty-one), she sets all the hottest trends (who knew baby tees were the wave of the future?), and she has survived numerous stalkers without so much as a run in her ultrahip thigh highs.

However, you, Tori, need some help. Sure, you're the daughter of Aaron Spelling and therefore the heiress to a huge fortune and the biggest mansion in Los Angeles. And yeah, you've had a pretty good acting gig with *90210* (not to mention at least one very entertaining TV movie).

But what's up with your *hair*? I mean, seriously, what are you thinking? Find a color and stick with it! Choose blond. Choose red. Choose black as midnight. But don't keep going back to that bottle of Clairol. The constant change makes us think you lack self-esteem, self-love, and an inherent sense of *self*.

And gain a little weight, why don't you? I could be wrong, but I'm willing to bet you a cappuccino that a personal trainer (and quite possibly some evil diet pills) is responsible for the fact that a small gust of wind could blow you straight into the Pacific Ocean.

Please shoot me an E-mail if you want me to expand on any of my comments.

Your devoted nonfan,
Tanya

At seven-fifteen Thursday morning Natalie jabbed the buzzer for Dylan's apartment several times in rapid succession. She needed his help—big time.

"Yeah?" Dylan's voice was slightly groggy over the intercom.

"It's me," Natalie yelled. "I need to come up."

Natalie leaned on the front door of the apartment building, waiting for Dylan to buzz her in. A moment later the door clicked open. Natalie started up the several flights of stairs that led to Dylan's apartment.

Dylan would know what to do. He always did. Sure, asking a girl's ex-boyfriend to help locate AWOL Girl in Question was slightly unorthodox. But Natalie needed to find Tanya, like, immediately.

As Natalie climbed the last flight of stairs she went back over the conversation she'd had with Mrs. Childes half an hour ago. . . .

Natalie smiled in her dream as she opened the small black box that Sam had handed her. She knew what was inside. The small diamond engagement ring they had picked out together.

"Yes," Natalie whispered. She leaned forward to kiss him, but his face had changed. . . .

Natalie's eyes popped open. Something had disturbed her near perfect dream. Something loud and obnoxious and rude. The telephone rang again. Natalie fumbled for the small Princess phone she kept next to her bed.

"Hello?" She glanced at the digital clock on her nightstand. Who had the nerve to call at six forty-five in the morning?

"Hi, Natalie. This is Alicia Childes."

Suddenly Natalie was wide awake. Early morning phone calls from the parents of friends never boded well. "Uh, hi, Mrs. Childes."

"Tanya didn't come home last night," Mrs. Childes said. Apparently she wasn't in the mood for small talk. "Is she there?"

Natalie's gaze traveled across her bedroom. Unless Tanya had sneaked into the van Lentons' house in the middle of the night and set up camp in the bathtub, she was definitely not on the premises. Which left Natalie facing a dilemma. Did she tell Mrs. Childes the truth or lie to cover Tanya's butt?

"She's here," Natalie said. She crossed her fingers. "We got home late last night, and I guess she forgot to call you."

"Can I talk to her, please?" Mrs. Childes didn't sound entirely convinced.

Natalie bit her lip. "Gee, she's, like, totally asleep," Natalie said as innocently as possible. "I *don't think a hammer to the head would wake her up. . . . Uh, you can probably hear her snoring in the background."* One lie led to another. And another. Ad infinitum.

"Just have Tanya call me the minute she wakes up," Mrs. Childes relented.

"Sure thing." Natalie had hung up the phone and jumped out of bed. So much for beauty sleep.

Dylan's door swung open. "What's going on, Nat?" Dylan was wearing a pair of faded Levi's— and nothing else. Natalie tried not to stare at his broad, tan chest.

"Tanya's missing," Natalie informed him. "She's probably with Major, but I don't have his number. . . . I sort of know where he lives, but it's a ways. . . ."

Dylan put his hand on Natalie's shoulder. "Relax, Nat. She's here."

Natalie's eyebrows shot up. "Tanya is *here?* In your apartment?"

Dylan stepped away from the door so that Natalie could come inside. She walked a few paces into the studio. On the far side of the room Tanya was sprawled out on Dylan's futon.

"Oh." Natalie wasn't sure what to say next. "That's, uh, great."

Tanya's eyes opened halfway. "Natalie? What are you doing here?"

"Saving you from getting grounded," Natalie told her. "Your mom called my house, looking for

183

you." Natalie didn't walk farther into the room. She was acutely uncomfortable. This scene was so . . . intimate.

Tanya sat up straight. "Ohmigod! I'm dead! I'm worse than dead."

"I covered for you. She thinks you spent the night at my house."

"Whoa . . . close call." Tanya flopped back down and sighed heavily. "I owe you one."

"Sorry you had to lie, Nat," Dylan said.

"That's okay. . . . I mean, it's not okay, but I understand. I mean, I don't know exactly what happened or anything. . . ." Her voice trailed off.

"Do you want some coffee or something?" Dylan asked. Apparently he wasn't alert enough to try and dissect Natalie's ramblings.

Natalie shook her head. "No, thanks. I'm going to head back home. . . ."

"See you later," Tanya called from the futon.

"See ya." Natalie backed out of the apartment and closed the door behind her.

As she started down the stairs Natalie tried to figure out what had just taken place. Tanya had spent the night at Dylan's. That much was obvious. And Dylan had answered the door sleepy and half dressed. The combination of facts pointed to one conclusion.

Good-bye, Major. Hello, Dylan. Tanya and Dylan had gotten back together. Natalie forced herself to smile. This information *should* make her happy. But for some reason she felt annoyed. And slightly . . . sad.

184

Tanya gave the cappuccino maker an enthusiastic bang. "Come on, baby, you can do it."

She was feeling good. No, she was feeling great. Last night she had restrained herself from doing something stupid, such as hooking up with a guy in order to prove to herself that she wasn't in love with Major. And in the process she had helped Dylan by listening to his mournful, lovesick speeches about Natalie.

Of course, she still had to inform Natalie that she and Dylan were *not* an item. But that little misunderstanding could be cleared up in a matter of seconds. As for Dylan and Natalie versus Sam and Natalie . . . who knew? Tanya had learned a long time ago that other people's hearts were indecipherable.

She hit the cappuccino maker again. Nothing happened. This machine was *not* cooperating. Tanya turned to the young guy who had just ordered a cappuccino. "Uh, how about a latte instead?" she asked him.

"Sure thing." The guy lounged against the counter to wait for his café latte.

Tanya hoped the rest of today's customers would be as laid-back as this guy. She didn't feel like spending the next eight hours arguing with cranky people about the fact that they couldn't get their cappuccinos.

185

"How about a cap for me?"

The hairs on the back of Tanya's head stood up as she listened to Major's deep, throaty voice. She finished pouring the latte and turned around to face him. "Hi, there."

Major looked beautiful. He was wearing a white T-shirt that looked fresh from its plastic wrapper and a pair of black jogging shorts. Tanya had never seen his legs before—it was a sight she wouldn't forget anytime soon. He crossed his arms in front of his chest.

"I came by your house last night."

"Really?" As if she didn't know that. After a grueling lecture about freedom-with-responsibility from her mom this morning, Mrs. Childes had casually mentioned that Major had stopped by—twice.

"And I was there this morning . . . early." The intense look in his eyes was causing Tanya's cheeks to burn.

"I was out," she said breezily.

Never mind that she had spent a full five hours telling Dylan how in love she was with Major and declaring that she would just die if she didn't see him in the next twenty-four hours. All Major needed to know was that Tanya had been out. Unavailable. Inaccessible.

"Were you with another guy?" He leaned so close that she could smell his Crest toothpaste.

"As a matter of fact, I was." She wasn't lying. She had been with a guy—technically. Tanya rang up the latte for her customer, who appeared to be observing this little scene with interest. "Do you have some kind of problem with that?"

Major shook his head. "Nope."

The customer handed Tanya two wrinkled dollar bills. "Keep the change," he said.

Tanya flashed him her most dazzling smile. "Come again."

"Were you with him all night?" Major asked. "This guy?"

Tanya shrugged. "And that's your business . . . because?"

"You're answering questions with questions." A small vein on the side of Major's forehead was visibly throbbing.

"You're jealous." Man, he was cute when he was jealous. Then again, Major was always cute.

He held out his hands in an I-surrender gesture. "Hey . . . I'm relieved. I mean, I'm the one who doesn't want to be nailed down into a June and Ward Cleaver type thing."

She pulled out The Smile again. "Great. Then we understand each other perfectly."

He nodded. "I guess we do."

Tanya allowed her eyes to drift back down to Major's legs. This day was shaping up nicely. She had taught Major a lesson, and she had the distinct feeling that he wasn't going to subject her to so many dateless evenings from now on.

Blue scanned the crowded café, searching for some sort of clue that would explain why everyone was acting like such a freak.

Over the last two hours Blue had noted the following: Dylan wouldn't speak to Tanya or Natalie—but he didn't appear to be angry with them, either. Sam was sitting in the booth by the window, staring most of the time at Natalie as if she were an alien who had just been dropped on earth by planet Zotron. Tanya kept bumping into things and muttering about how great it was that guys wore shorts in the summertime. Natalie seemed trapped in a world that was either very happy or very sad—every few minutes the expression on her face would change dramatically. As for Jason . . . he was alternately extremely friendly and extremely distracted.

Blue was just glad that she and Jason were more or less back on speaking terms. She had been a fool to get so worked up over Celia. If Jason wanted to date some imbecile, that was his affair (no pun intended) entirely. It wasn't like a few evenings with a redhead was going to jeopardize her own relationship with Jason. They were way past that.

Blue stared at the computer screen, surveying the list of new E-mail. There was something for Natalie. And there were a bunch of advertisements addressed to the café as a whole. But that was it.

"Mind if I sit down?"

Blue turned her head away from the computer screen and found herself staring straight at a pierced belly button. She looked up. Great. Celia, in the flesh—literally. "Jason is out on a break," Blue said. "I don't know when he'll be back."

Celia sat down at the computer next to the IBM that Blue was using. "I'm not here to talk to Jason."

"If you want coffee, I'd suggest ordering at the counter," Blue said. She looked back at the monitor and hoped Celia would go away.

"We need to have a little conversation about your friend and mine." Celia's voice was sweet, but Blue heard steely undertones.

She swiveled in her chair so that she and Celia were face-to-face. Whatever it was that Celia wanted to discuss, Blue wanted this whole encounter over and done with as quickly as possible. "I assume the *friend* is Jason. Unfortunately for you, I don't make a habit of talking about people behind their backs."

Celia flipped her long red hair over one shoulder. "I know you're in love with him."

Man, this girl really got to the point. She had caught Blue totally off guard. "I'm not in love with anyone."

"Right." Celia leaned back in her chair and gave Blue an intense once-over from head to toe. It felt a little like being a horse on an auction block.

"Listen, you're free to do whatever you want with Jason," Blue said. "But leave me out of it." There. That about said it all.

"Jason told me that you don't believe in romance and sex and all the other stuff that makes life worth living, but I don't believe him." Celia's voice was firm to the point of being scary. "I want you to keep your hands off him."

Blue would have gasped if she hadn't been so conscious that Celia was studying her face for any visible reaction to her last statement. Blue had just gone from being annoyed to being out-and-out furious. Who the hell did this girl think she was? And why was Jason divulging private information about Blue's personal life (or lack thereof)?

"I'll do whatever I want to do," Blue said in a low, abrasive voice. "Now why don't you go back to whatever alternative rock video you crawled out of?"

Suddenly the menacing look in Celia's eyes was gone. The shape of her face actually *changed* as she pasted on a Hello Kitty smile. "Did you hear me?" Blue said loudly. "Get lost."

Celia stood up . . . and held out her arms. "Jason!" she said sweetly. "I'm so glad you're back."

Blue turned around. Jason was giving her a cold, hard stare. "Me too," he said. "It didn't sound like you were just receiving a very warm welcome."

Celia slid into Jason's arms. "Don't blame Blue. I think she's just a little cranky."

Blood pounded in Blue's head. "Jason, this girl is insane. You should have heard what she was just saying to me." Wait a second. Was Blue actually *defending* herself?

"If you're still mad at me, that's fine," Jason said. "But don't take your anger out on Celia."

Blue leapt from her chair. This was sheer madness. "Tell me you're not serious." Jason had never taken someone else's side against her. Never.

"Why don't you go out and get some fresh air?" he suggested. "I'll cover for you for a while."

Blue hated him. And she hated *her.* She absolutely detested both of them. She never wanted to see either of their faces again. "I'll do more than get some fresh air," she shouted. "I quit."

As Blue stormed out of @café she heard several voices calling after her. But she didn't turn around. As of now, she was on her own.

Distraction. She needed distraction. All day Natalie had felt as if she were walking through thick San Francisco fog. Sam had kissed her twice in the alley behind the café. That had been nice. No, great. But she couldn't keep her mind off the image of Tanya asleep on Dylan's futon.

Tanya had told her, in between spurts of laughter, that Natalie had misread the situation. *There's*

191

absolutely nothing going on between Dylan and me,
Tanya had insisted. But Natalie wasn't sure she believed her. Where Tanya was concerned, it was very
rare that *nothing* was going on. Furthermore,
Natalie couldn't figure out why she cared.

Natalie clicked the mouse attached to the key-
board of the Gateway 2000. Blue had told her
there was an E-mail for her. Hopefully Blue hadn't
accidentally erased the message in her hurry to
storm out of the café.

A list of E-mail popped up on the screen. There it
was. A message for Natalie from DeliaB. Natalie
clicked on read. She couldn't wait to find out if Delia
Broderick had any connection to her mother's side of
the family. She started to scan the short note:

Natalie,
   I can't tell you how happy I am that you found
me. I always hoped this day would come, but now
that it's here, I'm even more excited than I thought I
would be. I promised your father that I would
never . . . well, I don't want to get into all that right
now. I was desperate to call you as soon as I read
your E-mail, but I decided that contacting you this
way first would be a better idea. You see, I did know
your mother. That is, I do know her. Your mother
isn't dead. She's alive and well and living in
Portland. I am your mom, Natalie. I love you . . .
and I can't wait to talk to you.

                              Love,
                              Mom

Natalie couldn't breathe. She couldn't see. She couldn't hear. Big black dots floated in front of her eyes. The blood from her head had rushed to her toes. Time had either stopped or it was rushing forward. This wasn't true. It was some kind of a sick joke. Some weirdo on the Internet messing with her mind.

Natalie tried to think clearly. This Delia Broderick from Portland obviously had her confused with someone else. Or she was an imposter. She thought Natalie's dad would give her money . . . or something. This was *not* true.

"Natalie? Nat?" Tanya's voice seemed to be coming from a million miles away.

Natalie felt Tanya's hands on her shoulders. "I can't . . . I can't . . ."

"What's wrong?" Tanya asked. "Are you okay?"

Natalie blinked. Everyone in the café was staring at her. Sam was walking quickly across the black-and-white tile floor, and Dylan seemed to have stopped a sale midring. Tanya's eyes were wide and concerned.

"I'm . . . I have to go." Natalie couldn't tell them about the E-mail. How was someone supposed to blurt out the fact that their own mother—who she had believed was dead—was alive after all?

And it wasn't true. There had been a mistake. A big, huge, gigantic mistake.

Natalie hadn't started to cry yet. She wasn't going to allow one tear to slide down her cheek until she talked to her father. And her sister. They would tell Natalie that the woman in Portland was insane. And then everything would be fine. Natalie would go back to the café and finish her shift. Tonight she would go out with Sam, and they would have a great time. And that would be that. The end of this horrifying episode in her life.

She was almost home. Just a few more steps. Natalie walked up the front path of the house she had lived in for almost as long as she could remember. It looked different somehow. Was it possible that she had been living a lie? No. No. She couldn't even contemplate the idea.

Natalie opened the front door. "Dad! Mia!" she shouted.

Her argument with Mia over Matthew Chance seemed as if it had been years ago. Right now Natalie wanted nothing more than to see her sister's face. The face of someone she could trust.

"Mia!" Natalie was screaming now.

Mia appeared at the top of the stairs. "What's wrong?"

Natalie started up the staircase. "Where's Dad?"

"Duh. He's at work." Mia leaned against the wall and crossed her arms in front of her chest. "Is there a reason you're screaming like a banshee?"

"I got a letter," Natalie said. She sat down on

194

the top step and dropped her head in her hands. "An E-mail."

"And?" Mia didn't sound impressed.

"There's a woman in Portland who claims to be our mother." There. She had said it.

Mia sank onto the step next to Natalie. "Delia Broderick." It was a statement, not a question.

Natalie's heart lurched. "Has she written you, too? Is she crazy?"

Mia shook her head. "She's not crazy, Nat."

Natalie saw the black dots again. "What . . . what do you mean?"

"Our mother isn't dead, Nat." Mia put her arm around Natalie's shoulders and hugged her close. "She's alive."

"No, she's not!" Natalie yelled. "You're lying!" She jumped up from the staircase. "I hate you!"

Tears poured down Natalie's face as she ran blindly into her bedroom. Mia was obviously lying. She wanted to hurt Natalie because Natalie was mad at her about Matthew Chance. Or maybe Mia was just evil. Natalie slammed her bedroom door shut and collapsed on her bed. She had to get ahold of her dad. He would tell her the truth. He would tell her that Mia and the woman in Portland were lying.

The door opened. Mia walked quietly into Natalie's bedroom. "Read this." She handed Natalie a single sheet of paper. "It's from our mother."

Natalie wiped the tears from her eyes. Her

heart pounded as she read the loopy, feminine handwriting.

"It's from her," Mia said. "I met Delia a few months ago when I was doing a photo shoot in Portland. . . . She's been sending me letters ever since." Mia brushed a tear from her own cheek. "I hate her so much, Natalie. . . . She abandoned us . . . all this time."

Natalie threw the letter aside. "It's true? It's really true?"

Mia nodded. "Our mom is alive, Nat."

Natalie closed her eyes. Mia was telling the truth. Delia Broderick was telling the truth. But her dad had lied. He had been lying to Natalie her whole life.

Everything had changed. Natalie's mother was alive, and nothing would ever be the same again.

About the Author

Elizabeth Craft is the author of many young adult novels, but *@café* is her first very own series. Ms. Craft is originally from Kansas City. Currently, she lives in a tiny studio apartment in New York's Greenwich Village. She enjoys reading romance novels, going to bad movies, and cruising coffee shops for cute guys.

Blue and Jason are methodically destroying their friendship. Sam's barely holding his family together. Tanya's totally lost it over Major. Natalie's whole world has been turned upside down. And Dylan's afraid he'll go crazy trying to hide his feelings for Natalie. Someone's about to reach the breaking point. But who?

DON'T MISS THE CHANCE
TO FIND OUT.
READ @CAFÉ #3:

Make Mine to Go

WARNING: CONTENTS
EXTREMELY HOT!

"I'm Buffy, and you are history."

BUFFY

THE VAMPIRE

SLAYER™

As long as there have been vampires, there has been the Slayer. One girl in all the world, to find them where they gather and to stop the spread of their evil and the swell of their numbers.

#1 THE HARVEST

A Novelization by Richie Tankersley Cusick

Based on the teleplays by Joss Whedon

Created by Joss Whedon

#2 HALLOWEEN RAIN

Christopher Golden and Nancy Holder

From Archway Paperbacks
Published by Pocket Books

1399-01

party of five™

Join the party!

Read these new books based on the hit TV series.

#1 Bailey:
On My Own

#2 Julia:
Everything Changes

**Available
From Archway Paperbacks
Published by Pocket Books**

POCKET
BOOKS

© 1997 Columbia Pictures Television, Inc. All Rights Reserved.

What's it like to be a Witch?

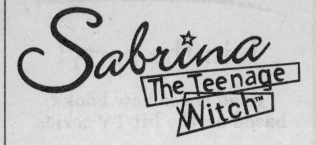

Sabrina
The Teenage Witch™

*"I'm 16, I'm a Witch, and I **still** have to go to school?"*

◆◆◆◆◆

#1 Sabrina, the Teenage Witch
by David Cody Weiss and Bobbi JG Weiss

#2 Showdown at the Mall
by Diana G. Gallagher

#3 Good Switch, Bad Switch
by David Cody Weiss and Bobbi JG Weiss

#4 Halloween Havoc
by Diana Gallagher

Based on the hit TV series

Look for a new title every other month.

From Archway Paperbacks
Published by Pocket Books

1345-03